OLD SPACEMEN NEVER DIE!

By
JOHN W. JAKES

I0617071

ARMCHAIR FICTION
PO Box 4369, Medford, Oregon   97501-0168

*For more information about Armchair Books and products, visit our
website at...*

www.armchairfiction.com

Or email us at...

armchairfiction@yahoo.com

A HATE THAT SPILLED ACROSS THE GALAXY

They were brothers…yes…but in name only. Each wanted the other dead—and they weren't too timid about pulling a trigger or sinking a knife. One commanded a powerful galactic fleet, the other commanded a fleet of murderous space pirates. When they met in battle, a wave of unimaginable bloodshed soon spread across the galaxy. And then there was the woman, the wanton woman whom both brothers wanted for reasons unknown even to themselves—the woman whose nakedness of body and rawness of character only fanned the flames of their hatred even brighter.

Famed author John W. Jakes spins an exciting, yet decidedly grim tale of bloody interplanetary conflict and intrigue. A story filled with hatred, love, lust, and death—all wrapped in the enigma of twisted human frailties.

FOR A COMPLETE SECOND NOVEL, TURN TO PAGE 79

CAST OF CHARACTERS

MATT CAIN

He commanded hundreds of spaceships. And he would use them to track down and kill his hated enemy—his own brother.

TIME

Blindly loyal to Matt Cain. He was part man, part metal—and he was old! But he was still the best first officer in the fleet.

MARCO CAIN

His bloodlust had transformed him into an interplanetary killer, the likes of which the galaxy had never seen before.

ARNA

Kind of a sleazy broad in many ways. Aging and overweight, yet there was something about her that was completely irresistible.

ORBECK

A good, disciplined officer that Matt Cain was thankful to have on board—especially when times got tough.

LACE FREDERICK

He knew all about the many illegal activities on the planet Blackrock, but the price for his information might be too high..

CHAPTER ONE
Massacre

THE SHIPS hung in the great dark—like clusters of silver coins flung on the black cloth of space. The suns of Galaxy Eighteen burned all around them, green and pale white and candle-flame red. The space lanes were silent, empty of the thunder of rockets. The ships, nearly a thousand of them, hung steady, waiting. The vortex cannons were manned. On the bulging bow of each ship were huge letters outlined in the faint luminescent glow of the guide lights.

The letters spelled, *Sol, Incorporated.*

In the chartroom of the flagship *Caliban I,* Matthew Cain paced restlessly along the catwalk that ran just inside the wide observation window. He watched his fleet with narrow gray eyes, moving with lithe, easy steps that held just the faint suggestion of a swagger. His brown hair was even more tangled than usual, left that way from the nervous movement of one of his muscular hands.

Below the catwalk, the astrogators sat at their high slanting tables, smoking and talking quietly. The instrument banks before them were dead, the rows of tiny lights dark. Like the ships, the astrogators waited, there in the high-ceilinged room under the light of the big ceiling illumination units.

On the catwalk, Matthew stopped pacing. He turned quickly to an older man with thin gray hair, who stood leaning against the rail with an air of quiet precision. The back half of the small man's skull was a curved plate, shining with a dull metallic glint.

"Give me a cigarette," Cain said sharply.

The little man fished one out of his tunic pocket and handed it over. Light flashed from the metal left hand that served in place of a real one. "You nervous, Matt?" he asked.

Matt threw back his cloak. The bloody lining shimmered. He struck a match on his boot and put it to the cigarette. "You keep your mouth shut," he said thickly.

The little man shrugged. "All right. Only I was just thinking, what if he doesn't come."

Smoke plumed from Matt's nostrils. His lips skinned back over his teeth and he laughed. It was not pleasant to see. "He'll come all right. He knows better than to try and play games with me. After all, I was raised with him."

"He's your brother," the little man agreed, fiddling with his belt. "If he's like you, maybe he won't come..."

Matt was watching space again. "I told you to shut your mouth," he said, taking a long pull on the cigarette. "I told you—" His voice trailed off. One arm came up, pointing.

"There, by God," he breathed. "There!"

THE LITTLE man, whose name was Time, peered over Matt's shoulder. Above the ships, another fleet could be seen, plunging down toward them. The jets flamed in the blackness, and there was a faint rumble, even within the flagship.

"He hasn't got more than two hundred ships," Matt said softly, watching the approaching fleet. "And they're tubs, all of them. Class eleven freighters, converted."

"Looks like he's got some vortex cannon rigged," Time commented, seeing the round openings along the sides of the ships.

"But we've got more." Matt's eyes were eager and full of strange hunger. "I just hope he starts something. We'll blow those tin cans of his from here to the Yellow Frontier."

Quickly, Matt turned to the rail and began calling orders. The astrogators put out their cigarettes hastily.

"Sound alert for the cannoneers," Matt yelled. "Full stations. Boarding parties ready with the fliers. Complete armament. Alert the captains of all ships."

The astrogators flipped switches on the banks of machinery. The small lights began to go on and off like blinking eyes, while the men at the slanting tables spoke orders into microphones.

Time caught Matt's arm. "I don't think you should go over there alone. He may want you to do just that."

Matt grinned. "If I'm not back in..." He glanced quickly at his wrist chron. "...thirty minutes, blow hell out of them. I'll be dead and it'll be too late to worry anyway."

"Matt, I wish you'd..."

The younger man flung off Time's hand. His voice grew hard. "You're in charge of this ship, Time. You're not in charge of me. If it wasn't for this command, you'd be getting your lungs eaten out in the dust mines. You'd be just another guy who got blown up and put back together with plastic and metal and wire. Remember that."

He turned away from Time, who licked his lips and stared at the floor. The photocell in the wall at the end of the catwalk buzzed and the elevator door slid open. Matt stepped in. It clanged shut. The tube carried him down into the iron bowels of the ship.

Matt anticipated the meeting. His fingers ran up and down the hilt of the dress rapier. Dress or not, it had a blade that was deadly. He laughed again, thinking how fine it would be if he could ram the blade through his brother's neck. But that would be too easy.

With a loud *spang*, the elevator door opened. Matt walked up a long narrow ramp, cloak flapping behind him. One of his officers, in a black cape and shock helmet, saluted.

"Where's the flier?" Matt asked.

"In the lock, sir."

"As soon as I'm out, beam their flagship. Tell them I'm on my way over."

"Right, sir." The officer vanished down another branch of the hallway.

Matt climbed through the small hatch of the cylindrical flier and used the automatic controls to close the inner door. The outer lock opened, sliding to one side. He pulled the control bar and the flier made its coughing roar, rising into black space.

THE AIR in the flier cabin was cold, but Matt did not notice. He was too caught up in the coming meeting. Behind him, he felt the tremendous power of his fleet. *His* fleet. The thought was good.

Signal sirens were screaming on the ship ahead. Red beacons circled in the dark. They saw him coming.

He picked out the flagship easily. It was a big vessel, but its sides were caked and rotted with rust. Carefully steering the flier, he watched the other ships. They deployed in three circles, one on top of the other. In the center of the middle circle hung the flagship. On its bow, two letters were splashed in purple phosphorous paint, mockingly: *MC.*

The flier slid through the airless black, up through the bottom ring of ships and toward the flagship. The lock gaped, spilling light. Matt guided the flier inside, waited for air to return, and stepped out.

The inner door opened. A beefy man with a dirty uneven brown beard and tremendous arms stood pointing a blaster at Matt's belly. His lips made a tiny malicious pink pucker.

"I'm the first mate to Cap'n Cain," he rumbled.

"He's expecting me?" Matt asked with faint sarcasm.

"That's right," came the reply, and with heavier sarcasm, "*sir.*"

They took an elevator upwards. When it came to a halt, the mate motioned him forward.

The room was fitted out as a lounge. There were thickly covered orchid divans, a heavy flowered rug from, Matt thought, Xenol in Galaxy Eleven, blond wood liquor cabinets. It showed a woman's hand, and a rather cheap one at that.

The woman was there, too.

She sat on one corner of a divan, holding a liquor glass. She was a big woman, with long legs and a full body. Her gown hung open to her waist, exposing large deep breasts. She looked at Matt over her shoulder. Yellow hair tumbled down loosely. Her lips were parted, red and wet. She peered at him out of gray eyes, with the peculiar dreaminess of half-slumber.

"You look like you just got out of bed," Matt said.

"I did," she said, frowning.

"Where's Marco?"

"He'll be here."

Matt wrinkled his nose at the cloud of musky perfume around her. A sound tape played somewhere, weird minor themes interspersed with kettledrums.

"I didn't know my brother went in for run-down mistresses," Matt said casually, sensing the dislike the woman felt for him.

She got up and walked to the liquor cabinet. She didn't look at him. A siphon hissed. "You *are* rotten, just like Marco told me," she said.

The mate jerked his shoulder. "Better watch out what you say to her. You aren't on your own ship now." The fat fingers had harsh, biting power as they gripped Matt's shoulder.

"Oh yes," he replied, "of course."

A door opened. Marco Cain walked in.

THEY STOOD looking at each other, the two men who had been born on Mars, back in Galaxy One of the Earthmen. They were a great deal alike, tall, well built, with Marco the heavier of the two. Both had black hair that was wild and tumbling.

Marco fixed himself a drink without saying anything. His uniform was a makeshift affair, the cloak patched and repaired in many places. He moved much as Matt did, but with a more deliberate slowness. But there was one thing the two men shared perfectly.

Hate.

Marco weighed the glass in his hand. "I got your message on Blackrock. You advertised very well. Every dive in the Galaxy knew you wanted to see me, and where."

"I've still got connections," Matt replied.

"I came because I want to know just exactly what you want," Marco said, seating himself and putting his arm around the woman. "This is Arna."

Matt ignored the introduction. "And I want to know what you're doing in Galaxy Eighteen."

"Seeing the sights." Marco took a drink. Arna rubbed her shoulder against him, head back, eyes closed.

Matt stared at the wall for a minute. A flag hung there, a white piece of cloth, painted with the same purple phosphorous letters that burned on the outside of the ship: *MC*.

"Marco, don't waste time."

"I'm not." He took another drink, deliberately.

"Lay it on the line."

Marco studied him. "All right. I hate you the way a man hates the worst things in his life, Matt. But I want to give you a chance. I'll get a hell of a lot more pleasure out of finishing you that way."

"Go on."

Arna lit a cigarette, passed it to him. Smoke climbed to the ceiling in the dim light. Matt kept one hand on his sword. The mate was unmoving, blaster on Matt's back.

"I was over in Galaxy Four for a while," Marco said. "Leading a mercenary army. Profitable. But I heard about you. Commander of the Sol Incorporated transport fleet in Galaxy Eighteen. Practically a dictator. How did you get the post?"

"By slaughtering more brigands than the last commander."

Marco waved his hand. "There's the point. The next in line has to be tougher than the last. I'm going to wreck you, Matt. I'm going to wreck the Sol Incorporated transport fleet until the big boys in Galaxy One crawl around and beg me to work for them, instead of fighting them. That way, I can relax." He looked at the woman. "We like relaxing, Arna and I."

She laughed softly, kissed him on the mouth, pressing against him.

"You're crazy, Marco," his brother said. "I found out what you want all right, but I know you can't win. You always want everything, just like you did when you were a kid. But this time you won't get it. You think you're such a damned big military man…"

Marco rose, face darkening. Keep quiet, Matt."

"Look at you," Matt roared. "Look at you, in this rotten wreck of a ship, with a fleet of run-down ore freighters, and a worn-out woman and old clothes and…*that.*"

HIS SWORD licked out before the mate could stop him. It rasped and tore through the flag on the wall, pulling it free. Matt let it hang on the point of his blade.

"Try and finish me, Marco. I wish you would."

He threw down the flag.

Marco held tightly onto his glass for a moment. Then his arm flashed backward and he threw it at Matt's head.

The mate jumped forward, clubbing at Matt with the blaster. Matt whirled, slicing downward with his blade. The mate screamed and the blaster dropped. The mate's sleeve began to darken with a long line of blood.

"I'm going back to my fleet and blow your ships out of space," Matt whispered. "Sol Incorporated keeps war rockets for pirates like you." He ran toward the elevator. The mate stumbled after him.

"Let him go," Marco yelled. "Remember this, Matt. You're finished..."

His voice drifted in the elevator. The closing door cut it off. No one tried to stop Matt. He clambered into the flier, waited till the lock opened automatically, and sent it roaring out into space.

His eyes searched upward. His brother's fleet was regrouping. The rockets made wisps of flame in the night of space. The flier shot away from the ancient ships, toward the shining war rockets of the Sol Incorporated fleet.

The leaders back in Galaxy One would make Matt a Trigalactic Commandant if he killed his brother. The thought was pleasant. But he couldn't help feeling just a bit shaken. Marco had been so damned confident.

He dialed the *Caliban I* on the flier beam set. The receiver buzzed and then the voice of the communications officer came in.

"Give me Time on the bridge," Matt ordered.

"Time, bridge," a voice said after a minute.

"Formation eight-three. Begin firing. Keep the *Caliban* back until I reach you. I want every one of Marco's ships out of the sky in an hour.

Time's voice was quiet as death. "They're already going."

"What the hell are you talking about?"

Almost as if he could see Matt with his eyes on his own fleet, Time said, "Look behind you."

Matt jerked around. His jaw went slack and he gagged. Marco's ships were...*disappearing.*

"In God's name..." Matt choked.

The old ships were nearly all gone. Only about twenty remained. And those few were vanishing. Not jetting away...*vanishing.* There were no trails of fire in the black to mark their passing. There was only a filmy white aura springing up around each of them, a wavering, as the line of the ships grew indistinct, and then space, sprawling with points of light where the ships had been.

Matt didn't talk. Until he had slammed the flier into the lock and run back to the chart room with fear gnawing great chunks out of his stomach, he didn't talk:

TIME STOOD in the middle of the chart room. The astrogators slumped listlessly over their tables, expectancy gone. There was nothing to fight any more.

"What happened to them?" Malt shouted.

Time pulled on his cigarette. "Don't you know?"

"Hell no. Those ships couldn't have faster-than-light drive. They're too old. Even we don't have it, and the *Caliban's* only been in service three years."

His voice echoed hollowly in the room. The astrogators watched him out of dispirited sunken pits of eyes.

Time blew out smoke. "Your brother's got teleportation."

Matt choked. "But...but that's illegal!"

"Not to men like Marco."

"Time, get a beam through to Venusburg, Galaxy One. Tell the Marshall that we've got to have a fleet of faster-than-lights right away."

"Check."

Matt's mind twisted and churned at the thought of the weapon his brother possessed. Instantaneous transportation to any point in the galaxy. Immeasurably dangerous...

One of the astrogators handed him a portable com receiver.

"Message from Transport Base, Planet one hundred four, Argon, Yellow Frontier Sector. Unidentified fleet appeared. That's the exact wording, *appeared.* Element of surprise overcoming immediate defenses. Request assistance."

Matt threw down the phone. His hand was knotted into a fist.

"Direct flight," he shouted at Time. "Argon, Yellow Frontier. Marco must have teleported his fleet there after I left him. I want every bit of power you can squeeze out of the rockets."

Time ran toward the main com room. Matt climbed to the catwalk, stood looking out of the observation window. The astrogation tables began to flash and hum once more.

A powerful trembling roar filled the *Caliban I.* The stars began to move, wheel in the heavens. Deployed around the flagship, Matt could see the war rockets, plunging like silver bombs through the cold silent night of Galaxy Eighteen.

Matt calculated swiftly. Three parsecs. Fifty-seven and six tenths trillion miles. Almost twelve hours...

The rockets made thunder. Fire burned from the rear of the fleet as it hurtled on.

Matt stayed in the chart room, thinking about Marco's teleportation. Teleportation was dangerous because of the unknown warps in space, but Marco would take the chance...*damn him...*

The ships plunged into the maze of planets and suns known as the Yellow Frontier exactly eleven hours later. One hour and fifteen minutes after that, the *Caliban* flashed down into the atmosphere of Argon while the remainder of the fleet hovered just outside the envelope of air.

Matt grew sick at his stomach. The great supply base, twenty miles on a side, was a ruin. Gigantic craters gaped where the storage sheds and tool shops had been. Blood still bubbled on the warm ground. Thousands and thousands of dollars of equipment, gone. Several thousand men gone...

It was morning, near dawn. Matt had the ship set down. He walked about in the wreckage, smoking. His cloak whipped in the wind. The sky was beginning to grow gold in the south. There were pieces of bodies scattered over the burnt ground. Girders made skinny bent fingers against the dawn sky.

Someone groaned in the wreckage. A tube repairman, a blue Martian, lay pinned under the corner of a metal beam. He asked for Matt's cigarette. Matt held it down to his lips. Just as the Martian inhaled, the beam creaked and the corner pushed into his stomach. The blue flesh tore. Greasy ichor welled onto the ground. Matt turned away quickly.

He walked toward the *Caliban,* picking his way through the ruins. The wind seemed colder. He stood looking up into the gold sky, seeing beyond it, to where Galaxy Eighteen lay spread out with its millions of worlds.

"All right," he said softly, his hate a quiet and terrible thing, *"we'll see who wins."*

He walked quickly back to the ship in the wind.

CHAPTER TWO
The Trail of Marco Cain

THE *Caliban I* raised on her jets from the atmospheric envelope of Argon and rejoined the rest of the fleet. Matt went to his cabin and called for a meeting of all his captains. The fliers darted toward the flagship like angry insects and, presently, the one hundred or so officers sat restlessly in a small auditorium.

On the stage, Matt walked back and forth while he explained the situation. When he had finished, there was only a faint rustle of talk.

"We'll have to watch out," Matt told them. "I'm going to have Time, here, issue your orders. You'll be assigned in groups of three war rockets each to one of the main cargo lanes. We haven't any way of telling where my brother will strike next. I don't doubt that he'll try to stop some of our big shipments, and we'll have to be prepared. But that still leaves the basic problem unsolved."

Time got up from his chair, raising his left hand. It flashed metallically in the light. "What do you want?" Matt said hastily.

"Well," the little man replied quickly, "I think something more ought to be done. I mean besides watching the space lanes. Your brother practically kicked our faces in the mud down on Argon."

A rolling angry growl came from the lips of the captains. It rose and echoed around the auditorium, full of throbbing hatred. Matt threw his head backward and laughed. His mouth twisted sarcastically. "So you thought I was just going to sit on my behind and wait for him to finish us? Not exactly." He laughed again.

"What's the plan?" somebody called from the back of the room. It was a captain from Prbno of Galaxy Seven. The young android blinked his three square eyelids and waited.

"Marco said he got my message about wanting to see him on Blackrock." Matt paused, waiting for the effect to strike. There was a chorus of ahs, sibilant and anxious.

"That means he must have landed there. If he landed there, he had to go to one of the cities, or he'd never have gotten the message. My guess is, he chose Elfharin. And that's where I'm going to look for him."

"How many ships do you want?" a commander from Rigel called.

Matt drew his breath in slowly. "None. I'm going alone."

The captains jumped up, pushing over chairs, scrambling, yelling their protests. Time ran up on the stage and began arguing, shaking his artificial hand up and down until it made a steady blur.

"Keep quiet!" Matt yelled, raising his arms.

"You know what kind of a place Blackrock is," Time shouted, "and Elfharin…if they ever found out who you were, you'd be pulled to pieces. You can't go."

Matt shouted again, *"Keep quiet!"*

His face was livid as the shouting died. "I'm going alone, in a flier. The *Caliban* will lie about a thousand miles outside the atmosphere, with light shields up so they can't detect us. That's final. Get back to your ships, and wait for orders as to what space lanes you're to take."

Someone called attention loudly. Boots snicked together. Matt raised his sword in front of his face, brought it down sharply. Then the captains started out of the hall, pushing toward the doors.

Matt turned to Time, his face carved in a strange, almost sadistic grin. "For all his talk, my brother's made some mistake, somewhere. By God, I'll find it. Now listen to me, Time. Draw up a list of the principal shipping lanes. Alert the Central Depot on Merthor to brief all ships on battle precautions, and send a report back to headquarters in Galaxy One. Assign the war rockets to various lanes the way I said. I'm going down to the Concealment Lab. When the rest of the fleet goes, set the course for Blackrock."

DOWN IN the iron bowels of the ship, the men were preparing for jet-off time. They worked busily behind the lead shields, tending the huge piles that chained up force and drove the flagship. Matt smiled in satisfaction, and then he remembered the corpses and the wreckage in the gold dawn of Argon and his face darkened.

The Concealment Lab was a big, barn-like room on a lower deck. There were banks of setup that controlled the screens that kept out light rays. There were great nets for covering the ship while it lay on the ground. The sharp, not unpleasant aroma of paint filled the entire room.

In one corner were several large chairs. A furry man with great pink-faceted eyes, dressed in the uniform of *Sol, Incorporated,* sat lazily in one of them, chewing on a fibrous green weed.

"Get off your can, Forg," Matt said.

Forg jumped up, knocked his heels together and said in his purring voice, "Yes, sir, Commander Cain."

Matt heaved himself into the chair, closing his eyes. He was tired. But the job was only started.

"Personal disguise this time, Forg. Slash my face. Give me a couple of scars...um let's say the left eye socket empty not much hair. And get out some old clothes. Tunic, cloak, everything. Disreputable. You understand."

18

"Perfectly, sir."

Matt waited. The needle slid into his cheek, and coldness crept through his facial muscles. Soft darkness pulled at his brain. He let himself fall into it.

When he opened his eyes, Forg held up a mirror proudly. Matt looked at himself. The plastic pigment was now a part of his skin, and could be removed only by another member of Forg's race. There were two raw scars, on his forehead and across his right cheek, and his eye socket was a ragged hole with crusty brown edges. His skin seemed to have an almost invisible coat of filth on it.

"All right," Matt said. "Now the clothes."

A few minutes later, he inspected himself in the long mirror. He had changed swords, using now a thick-bladed saber. There was a dagger on a chain around his neck and a blaster strapped beneath his armpit. His boots were black, dirty. The cloak was torn. A scarf of Callistan dream silk was knotted around his neck, and hung raffishly down his shirtfront.

Matt smiled, and the grotesque figure in the mirror seemed to be making its mouth writhe. Forg rubbed his furry brown hands together. His pink eyes were proud and full of a thousand small fires. He purred gently.

Nodding approval, Matt left the shed-like room and took the elevator back up. He could feel the careening motion of the jets. The *Caliban* was flashing through the dark light-years to Blackrock.

He went back to his cabin, put in a call to Time on the bridge.

"Pull up a thousand miles off Elfharin. Have my flier ready. Tell the repair crew to bang it up a little, burn off the Sol markings. I'm going to sleep. Wake me a quarter-chron before rendezvous. The other ships get off all right?"

"Assignments completed," Time replied. "Listen, Matt..."

Matt yawned. He flopped down on the bed and yanked the red rope. Sleep gas began to fill the chamber.

"Didn't I tell you to keep quiet once today?" he said thickly. The lights dimmed slowly and died altogether. Closing the com connection, he pulled the curtains around the bed and turned over onto his stomach, letting the warm cloying vapor carry him into fantastic swirling lands of sleep.

His last thought in the drugged darkness was, *I may not get any more sleep for a long, long time....*

THE FLIER, suitably damaged, lay in the airlock. Matt climbed into the cockpit.

"Where's Time?" he said to the officer standing by.

"I don't know, sir."

Matt narrowed his good eye. "He called me from the bridge."

"I suppose he's still there, sir," the officer said helpfully.

"Yeah. I suppose he is. I'll be back presently." His laugh was short and bitter. He slammed the cockpit closed. The lock doors clanged. The controls responded under his hands and the flier shot forward into space. Rapidly the *Caliban I* became lost in the dark. Her lights shone dimly. Then they were gone. That would mean the protective screens had gone up.

Matt concentrated on his course. Blackrock lay ahead, a single small planet revolving around a red dwarf star. Continents slowly became clear. Matt made out the volcanic highlands. Somewhere down there was Elfharin, the toughest city. Marco would go to the toughest city.

Abruptly, he swept the saber from its sheath, sprang out of his chair and crouched, peering into the dimness of the flier cabin. A voice had spoken his name. The flier jet made a solitary whisper. Matt waited, the cabin control lights throwing soft reflected radiance on the sword blade.

Time walked out of the shadows.

"I couldn't let you come alone," he explained sheepishly, fingering the plate in his skull. "I decided I'd better..."

Deliberately Matt slid the blade back into place. He walked forward, grunted softly and slugged the little man in the belly. Time doubled over. Matt clubbed his neck. Time groaned and rolled on the floor. His metal hand made a ludicrous clanking sound when it struck.

"Get up," Matt said.

Time got up and Matt hit him again, this time on the jaw. The little man leaned against a locker, gasping for air.

"One thing you've got to learn," Matt told him. "That's to follow orders. None of my men, not even you, are going to disobey my orders."

"I left Orbeck on duty," Time protested, wiping a little dribble of blood from the corner of his mouth. "Orbeck's a good man."

"Just remember, don't disobey my orders again. Right now I'm stuck with you. So keep quiet and do what I tell you. Understand?"

"Sure," Time muttered, with just a faint trace of tiredness. "Oh sure, I understand."

Matt turned back to the controls, ignoring Time. The flier was into the atmosphere of Blackrock. Below, Elfharin, the City of the Hill, rose on the slope of a mountain. The volcano chain spread across the jumbled land as far as Matt could see. Yellow fire and smoke belched from the conical towers of stone.

Matt set the flier down on the rocket field just below the city. He pushed a triangular coin from a bag tied at his belt into the meter. To Time he said, "You wait here. Watch for me. If I'm running, get the jets going, and fast. And that's an order."

He threaded his way through ancient rockets with patch plates scarring their rusty sides. Beyond the field, he walked up the hill and into the city of Elfharin.

IT WAS twilight. Red, bloody-film twilight. It was always twilight in Elfharin. One side of Blackrock was constantly lost in dark as it revolved around the red dwarf. The other side was seared desert. And here, it was always the half-world between darkness and the day.

Elfharin lay on the side of a great mountain. The mountain rumbled deep inside itself and blossomed with yellow fire that made the air sulfurous and hot. The city was built in terraces. Matt climbed through narrow alleys smelling of garbage and lit by small oil lamps in the windows of the plaster buildings. Water dripped down over the steps, carrying with it filth and refuse of a hundred races.

Elfharin was an outcast's city on an outcast's planet. Here came the hunted men, watching the stars for pursuit, faces burned by jet blasts, hands ready to grab and kill. Matt felt that of all the cities in the twilight zone of Blackrock, Elfharin would be where Marco would stop.

The lower terraces of the city were relatively deserted. Shadows moved in doorways. There were occasional shouts. Once the volcano flamed, high above, and Matt saw a dead woman in a doorway with her neck slashed. She lay there, eyes shining in the mountain fire. Matt hurried on.

The upper terraces were teeming. Some kind of festival was in progress. Musicians played somewhere, and men and women chanted and danced on the flagstones between the buildings. The small plaza to which Matt came at last was full of beings from many worlds. Their costumes made butterfly splashes of color, and the chant lifted and filled the sky. On top of one of the buildings, a Terran woman wearing only a skirt swayed drunkenly and sang in a high powerful voice, adding a note of keening madness to the whole frantic celebration.

Matt threaded his way through the crowd. His eyes caught a sign above a door. *Outpost Inn.* He pushed past a group of dancers and went inside.

It was a small shop. Men sat at one table, bearded, big-bodied men, drinking. A round fish belly-white Globular from Galaxy Two was behind the bar, polishing six bottles with his twelve tentacles.

Matt walked over to the bar. "Can I get some information?"

The Globular set down all six bottles and spread his tentacles, suckers down, on the bar. His round mouth opened and a wheezing came forth. Matt had to lean close to catch the words.

"What type of information does the Earthman wish?"

"I'd like to find out about something. Who could I see? It would have to be someone who knows every one of the illegal activities in the city." Matt allowed his mouth to screw up and winked broadly with his one good eye."

"That would be Lace Fredrick," came the reply. Four tentacles waved at the table of men. "There."

Matt put down one of the triangular coins and went over to the table. The men, seven of them, stopped drinking. They watched him, hands hovering at the edge of the table. From the plaza came the frenzied singing, the shouting, the high soprano voice.

"Lace Fredrick?" Matt asked quietly.

ONE OF the men got up. He was dressed like the others, in rough tunic, breeches and boots, but he was subtly different. He had a thin face and close-cropped blond hair.

His blue eyes were full of innocence and cleverness. He knotted a lace handkerchief in one slender hand. He might have been young or old.

"Yes?" he said. His voice sounded almost like a woman's.

"I want to talk to you," Matt replied.

"Charming," Lace Fredrick commented wryly. "Let's step into the back room, shall we?"

He moved ahead of Matt, gracefully, like a dancer in the video ballet. But there was a subtle repulsiveness above the movement, and Matt thought of a silicon snake, brittle and swaying and infinitely deadly.

Lace Fredrick closed the door to the back room and sat down at a table after lighting the small blue radiant lamp in the wall.

Matt sat down opposite him. "I want information," he said again, taking the bag of coins from his belt and setting it down on the table. There was a clinking rattle.

"That sounds adequate," Lace Fredrick said. He waved his handkerchief aimlessly. His other hand was in his lap. "Just exactly what kind of information did you wish?"

"I'm looking for a man named Cain," Matt said.

Lace Fredrick pursed his pretty lips. "Not Matthew Cain, Galaxy Commander for the Sol Shipping Fleet?"

Matt laughed shortly. "Hell no. I don't like men that keep me from making a living."

"Oh," said Lace Fredrick very softly.

"'I heard that Marco Cain, his brother, was recruiting some kind of fleet here," Matt said carefully, watching the other man's face. "I heard that he could use good fighting hands."

"You heard correctly, but unfortunately the fleet has gone. Some time ago."

Matt felt a sudden rush of inward triumph. His idea that perhaps Marco had secured his ships and men here, on promise of booty, had been correct.

"You don't know where I can catch up with him, do you?"

Lace Fredrick studied the wall behind Matt's head. "No, not really. I heard that he has a supply station on Set, along with quarters for his mistress. Two valuable properties."

"What part of Set?" Matt asked eagerly. "I have a flier..."

"Near the Ruined Temples of the Pear Worshippers, I believe," Lace Fredrick replied. "But I don't think that would be of any benefit...*Matthew Cain.*"

Matt's hand darted for the saber hilt.

"I wouldn't," Lace Fredrick said. "I have had a blaster on your stomach for quite some time." His other hand came up, and the ugly snout of the weapon thrust at Matt's head.

"Put down the blade," Lace Fredrick said affably.

Matt put it on the table. "How in hell..." he began.

The other man pulled open his tunic, laughing. There was a black T branded into the flesh.

"Telepath..." Matt breathed. "Of all the kinds of two-bit killers I had to run into, it had to be a telepath!"

"I'm extremely sorry," Lace Fredrick said with faint mockery. "I think you had better turn around."

Matt turned, reaching for the throat of his tunic. He took a low dive for the floor. Lace Fredrick fired. The wall smoked and there was a loud puff. By that time, Matt had the dagger from inside his tunic. He jerked the chain. It bit his neck and broke. He threw it as Lace Fredrick was swinging the blaster down toward his head.

The knife buried itself in Lace Fredrick's right eye. His scream keened upward and he fell across the table, the blood running down his face.

Matt grabbed the saber and jerked the door open. In the main room, Lace Fredrick's friends were up from their table, coming toward him. He swept up one of the tables, grunted, and tossed it across the room. It caromed into the men, throwing them backward. Matt was running toward the door, kicking over other tables behind him.

THE SQUARE was still noisy with singing and laughter. Matt pushed through the milling crowds, fighting them, kicking them out of the way, swearing. The laughter and music was horrible in his ears.

Across the plaza from the Outpost Inn, he stopped in the shadow of a pillar. The men were crowding through the door, searching for him. He wanted to see which direction they would take.

High above, beyond the terraces of buildings reaching toward the misty red sky, the volcano roared and erupted. Yellow brilliance washed over the square. Matt winced as the light filled the shadow in which he stood for a few moments. Across the square, one of the men saw him. They pushed their way through the mob.

He ran, away from the noise and the light and the music. He stumbled down the dark alleyways, over the steps dripping with water, toward the bottom of the hill. He heard boots pounding behind him. They could hear his footsteps, he assumed. His chest hurt and he breathed with effort.

Stumbling, he picked himself up. His breeches were soaked and dirty. His feet felt terribly heavy. He was running down a long flight of steps, in the dark.

The volcano flamed again. He cursed as the light swept over him. Renewed shouting split the air behind him. A blaster exploded and a piece of plaster wall crumbled to nothing near his head.

He dodged around a corner. A woman whispered from a doorway. Jerking himself to a halt, he moved into the shadows, put his arm around her and kissed her hard on the mouth. She felt fat and sloppy, but he kept on kissing her, and hoped to God that the volcano wouldn't flame again.

The men came running down the street. They clumped past, shouting angrily, swearing, only one of them looking in the doorway. They hurried on without stopping. Matt kept her mouth on his, not letting her go, until their pounding boots died away and only the music and the confusion from the higher terraces filled the air.

Matt pushed her away. She moaned and rubbed her body against him. He ran from the doorway and down another alley.

On and on, for endless miles of stairs, Matt ran. He leaned against the walls, practically falling down the steps. His mouth went open and closed in great gulps, gasping for air. At last, the ground leveled and he came out from among the last straggling buildings. Walking shakily, he moved through tumbled boulders toward the flier field.

Time saw him coming and lifted the flier a foot off the ground. Matt clambered inside, slid the cockpit closed.

"Get back to the *Caliban*," he said. "Fast."

Time nodded, jerking back the control bar. The flier went almost straight up. The mountains tilted insanely, the volcano seemed to shoot out a stream of fire along a horizontal plane. The red misty air began to darken, and at last they broke out into outer space.

Matt worked with the com set. He contacted Orbeck, the officer Time had left in command of the flagship.

"I'm coming in. Have the guide lights on."

"Right, sir. We got a beam from headquarters back in Galaxy One. They give you full authority, and they say if you can stop your brother, they'll make you a Tri-galactic Commander."

Matt tried to laugh and could not. But his deformed face was bunched and twisted into dreadful humor. "That's all I want," he said in a croaking voice. "Law and order and all the rest of that crap, all we want is to get someplace. Isn't that right, Orbeck?"

"Yes, sir," said Orbeck respectfully.

Matt turned off the set. Time was watching him. He turned his head quickly.

Matt kept on smiling. Far out in space, the tiny points of the *Caliban I* guide lights winked on. He knew which way he was going, now.

He knew which way he was going, to get his brother.

CHAPTER THREE
The Woman and the Bombs

ONCE BACK in the *Caliban*, Matt had Forg remove the plastic pigment. He went to his cabin, washed his face to remove the feeling of dirt, and drank a third of a pint of liquor. Then he went to the chart room.

One of the beam types was clacking out a message. Time bent over it, watching. Matt joined him, saw the paper coming forth, heard the clatter of the keys. His eyes had been dull and heavy, but now they burned, as he read the message.

From Sol Inc Transport Base, Pl Octov, City Augberg, Gal Eighteen. To Mt Cain, Cmndr Gal Eighteen, Caliban One, Somewhere in space. Unidentified fleet attacked cargo fleet containing valuable shipments of iridium one hour out from launching. Three convoy war rockets destroyed. Cargo ships entered, all crewmen forced through air locks into outer space. Iridium taken aboard raiding ships marked with purple MC on hull. Cargo ships evidently blown up, as have not been heard from. Early report said raiding ships appeared in space. Repeat, appeared. No survivors located. End message.

The machine stopped its noisy clatter. Matt could almost see his brother's men forcing the crewmen out into the airless void without space suits. He could almost see the bodies bursting like soft pulpy mushrooms.

He beckoned Time away from the machine, passed him a cigarette.

"Did you learn anything at Elfharin?" Time asked.

"Not a lot. Only one thing that might be of use. Marco is supposed to have a supply base on Set, near the Temples of the Pear Worshippers. Know where it is?"

Time shook his head. "But we can check it easily enough in the Galaxy Coordinate File."

"You'd better do it," Matt told him. "It's about the only approach we've got. Fix a course for Set. We'll take a look at this place. That's...let's see..." He paused to calculate.

"A long way," said Time. "Almost all the way across the Galaxy."

"Put the reflection screens on the outside of the ship so we'll shoot back the light when we land. That's about all for now."

Time knocked his heels together and walked off.

Matt went back to his cabin and finished the remainder of the pint of liquor. Then he took the elevator to the recreation deck and watched the latest telefilms for several hours. The ship was plunging through space and he needed rest. He took a shower, sat in the pneumatic massage room for a while, changed uniforms and returned to the bridge.

THE NEXT several hours were spent in loud and angry debate with Time over the best possible means of checking Marco.

At the end, Matt threw the slide rule down on the table. "Damn it, we *can't* know where he's going to strike next. We've got pitifully few ships, and we've got to take our chances until we can get in a crippling blow."

A loudspeaker crackled and a voice announced, "Position, five hundred miles outside the atmosphere of Planet Set."

Matt unhooked a microphone from the edge of the slanting table. "Put up the screens."

"They're already up, sir," the loudspeaker announced.

"Are we above the Ruined Temples of the Pear Worshippers?"

"Correct, sir."

"All right, mister." The rumble of jets was temporarily reduced to a low whine. Matt looked around. The astrogators listened eagerly, eyes excited, full of hunger for a chance to strike back. "I want two hundred men with riot guns in Lock A when we land. What's the terrain like?"

"Heavy jungle, sir."

"Jungle, eh. Well, make it about a mile from the ruins."

"Yes, sir." The voice boomed from the loudspeaker, shaking and anxious for the next command.

Matt said sharply, *"Take her down."*

The mighty explosion of the atomics rocked the chart room. Matt clung to the table until the gravity neutralizers came on. The push of deceleration stopped.

"Now I'm ordering you to come with me," Matt said to Time. "Orbeck in command," he bawled.

A beefy man on the catwalk high above slapped his heels together and waved.

In Lock A, the two hundred men were assembled, smoking and jostling one another. There was a gentle bump.

"Let's hope they didn't hear the jets," Matt said, slipping into a gray rubberized suit. "I don't think Marco's boys would know about things like reflection shields. If they looked for a ship to go with the sound, they wouldn't see a thing but sky." He laughed shortly, glancing around the assembled men.

"What's it like out there?" he asked.

A slight Oriental pushed his way into the crowd. "Little oxygen, sir. Helmets will be required. It is early morning, according to the rotation charts. Very warm. It would be better to plug in the cooling units," he finished crisply.

Matt studied him. "What's your name?"

"Lee, sir. Moy Lee, Atmospheric Control Officer, third class."

Attaching the cooler pack to his belt, Matt said, "You'll be second class before long, Lee. I like men who know their business."

Lee smiled from brown parchment cheeks and slipped the shining bowl of his helmet over his head. Matt put on his own helmet, called for order in the inter-suit microphone. He held up the heavy round-snouted riot gun in one gloved fist.

"See this? If we can find any of Marco's men, we're going to use them. Deploy in fourteenth combat formation. *Now open those doors!*"

THE LOCK swung ponderously open. Matt went first, leaping off the edge of the landing stage. It was a drop of six feet. He landed running, Time right behind him. The ship had smashed a neat hole in the jungle. Matt ran forward, scrambled over a bent tree trunk and slithered on his belly, waiting. Time came up beside him. Matt took in the situation. The men were already on the ground, the scouts somewhere ahead in the tangled growth. Behind them, the trees seemed unbroken. There was no *Caliban I.*

The jungle was dark and wet, filled with twisting moisture vapors. Loud inane screeches of fantastic blue birds with transparent fan-like wings filled the headphones. The cooling unit whispered silently. Drops of icy water rolled from Matt's armpits.

Far overhead, the trees pointed up to a morning sky like a sheet of polished silver. Matt's face was in a clump of saw-edged fuschia grass. He moved his left leg. There was a sound of sucking mud.

"Scout team reporting," a voice said in the phone.

"Proceed," Matt whispered.

"We're at the edge of the Temples. There's a big clearing. The Temples make a wall around it. We can't see what's inside. There are signs of habitation, though, and a part of the ground looks like it's been burned by jets."

"Can you see any men?" Matt asked tensely.

"None at all, sir."

"We'll come forward. Get off the line."

There was a short buzz. Matt spoke into the mike. "On your feet. Move forward in formation. Deploy along the edge of the clearing. Await further orders."

He closed the switch with his teeth, got to his feet. Time followed. They moved deeper into the forest, riot guns at ready. The two hundred spread out and walked slowly, boots sucking in the mud, like so many gray corpses in the humid empty world of the forest. The fan-winged birds dipped and circled and screamed.

It was a mile to where the trees ended. Matt pushed forward on his stomach, looked out. The Ruined Temples of the Pear Worshippers were great fallen towers of brown stone, each one topped with a shimmering bronze artifact that resembled the Terran fruit. Nothing moved. Only the birds wheeled in the silver sky, making their mad shrieking noise.

Matt tensed. The whole scene was too deserted. Beyond the brown towers could lie...anything.

"Scouts forward," he whispered. "On the run."

A line of fifteen gray-suited men broke from the trees, crouching low, racing toward the buildings. About a hundred yards from the first wall, they began to vanish. There was a series of loud explosions. White clouds shot through with streaks of fire mushroomed from the ground. Screams echoed in the phone.

The scouts were blown to pieces.

Matt felt himself retch. The smoke floated away. Pieces of gray rubber, fragments of a twisted riot gun, blood, half an arm, all these were on the ground.

"They've got the place mined," Matt whispered. "We can't get in…"

"Battle formation," Time whispered. "That's the way, Matt. Let's try to make it."

MATT GOT to his feet, huddled behind a tree, peering out. He gestured. The scene remained unchanged. No sign of life. Only the birds screaming and flapping their invisible wings. He said, "Who are we going to fight?"

Time sagged. "Matt, the men are restless. They've got to have…"

"You keep the men here. I'm going to look the place over myself." He clutched the riot gun, moved off through the fringe of trees, circling the temples.

The brown buildings ran all the way around the clearing. On the side opposite the position of his men, Matt paused. The breath came hard in his chest. There were footsteps coming rapidly through the forest.

Matt's mouth smiled, but his eyes behind the helmet were frigid. He braced the riot gun on his hip, throwing off the safety. The footsteps came closer, crashing through the undergrowth.

Here at last was something you could fight. Here was something you could aim at, fire at. You could watch the red fireball spiral lazily, striking the person, burning the flesh off the bones and then burning the bones themselves.

The footsteps were a hundred yards away from Matt, on the edge of the clearing. He closed his finger around the firing trigger.

Abruptly, he jerked the barrel upward as he pulled the trigger. The fireball popped from the end of the gun, headed upward over one of the towers toward the forest.

Matt ran forward. The runner turned, raised hand to mouth.

Matt grabbed her and held her tightly.

It was Arna, the woman from Marco's ship, and she was naked.

Her soft heavy body shone in the sunlight. She fought his grip. Matt slung the riot gun over his shoulder and twisted her arm behind her back.

"Now," he breathed, opening the communication vent in the suit so she would hear him, "what's going on here?"

He watched her eyes carefully. He figured her to be the type of woman who would play in the safest direction, no matter what it was. Right now, he had her.

"I was bathing in a pool. I heard the explosions..."

"How can you breathe?"

"This box around my neck." It was a small tan affair, hanging on a chain between her breasts. "It sets up a portable oxygen field and neutralizes the mines, for at least an hour. That's what Marco said."

"There are mines all over?"

She nodded quickly. "Oh yes. Even inside the ring of temples. That's where all the supplies are stored, drums of fuel, weapons..."

"The teleportation unit?"

"I don't know," she said evasively.

He bent her arm behind her back. *The teleportation unit?"*

"No...I...it's on Marco's flagship please...stop..."

He relaxed his grip a little. "What are you doing here?"

She tried to smile. "Marco said women don't belong when there's work to be done. He..."

"You can stop the act," he said coldly. "Where is Marco now?"

"I don't know," she said angrily. "He doesn't tell me everything."

"And the men that guard the base? I assume that there are men guarding it, since you're here."

She sensed the contempt in his tone, coughed once and spat at him. He wiped the saliva from his helmet with his free glove. "You'd better tell me."

"Out somewhere." She gestured to the jungle. "Hunting fresh food."

"You'd better keep that little machine turned on. We're going inside, and I wouldn't like to have you killed. Neither would Marco."

She said something obscene. He pushed her roughly ahead of him. They clambered over fallen pillars, through the dim interiors of the old brown buildings. There were empty altars, stained with the bloods of many races. Finally they came forth into the sunlight.

THE AREA enclosed by the temples was like a great amphitheater. There were tents erected, packing cases stood tier on tier, round dark green fuel drums, holding the liquid chemicals used by Marco's non-atomic ships, lay in rows.

"Very nice," Matt commented. "And there are mines, even in here?"

"So I'm told." There was sudden hatred in her voice. Matt looked at her naked body in the silver sun-glare and felt contempt and pity. Her beauty was fading, and there was little else left, it seemed. Someday Marco would get rid of her. But now...

"I've got an idea, Arna," Matt said. "A fine idea." He jerked her along after him, toward the opposite side of the camp. As they emerged from the jumble of temple buildings, Matt saw Time gaping at them from the edge of the trees.

"Keep her," Matt ordered Time. "She may make a very nice hostage. Now..."

Time clawed the air behind Matt, pointing. *"Ship!"* he yelled.

"Marco's men?" Matt asked hurriedly.

"Yes," Arna replied triumphantly. "Yes, Marco's men."

The rocket, a small class-eleven freighter, began to lower toward the charred area of the clearing.

Matt twisted the chain around Arna's neck, pulled loose the tan box. "How much of a human body, without this contraption, would set off the mines in the center?"

She didn't answer.

He pulled the riot gun off his shoulder, pressed the round muzzle against her white stomach. She shivered. Her voice was very faint. "Not much. They're all over."

The ship crunched down. The port swung open. About a dozen men got out, stretching lazily, hefting the carcasses of some strange breed of animal. Matt spoke into the suit phone, "Everybody keep quiet."

He handed Time the riot gun, with instructions to kill Arna if she made any sound. He knew, somehow, that she would not even try.

Recklessly, he began to run across the clearing. One of Marco's men spotted him, dropped the animal carcass, reached for his blaster.

MATT RAN on, dodging around the rusty bulk of the ship, tan box clutched tightly in one fist. He bent low and scooped up a fragment of arm, the remains of one of his men. He was too afraid to feel revulsion.

Scrambling through the maze of the wrecked temples, he heard the men coming after him. There was a crooked stairway, leading up into damp darkness. He ran up there, emerged on a parapet that ran all the way around the tower.

The men broke through the ruins into the center of the clearing. He could see the tan boxes hanging around their necks. They searched the ruins with their eyes. One of them cried out hoarsely and pointed. A blaster roared. Part of the wall behind him sheared away in a clattering of dust and rock.

Matt drew himself up, whipped back his arm and threw the piece of human flesh and bone out and down into the center of the supply clearing. There were shouts of terror. He dashed around the parapet, crawled over it and jumped out into space.

The long, long fall, and then he smashed to the ground in a tumbler's roll. He came up running. Behind him, there was a slow rising noise, as of great mountains being thrown together.

Time and his men watched fearfully from the forest edge. The brown temples began to totter. A falling stone glanced off Matt's shoulder. Pain jarred through his body, but he ran on.

As he passed the rocket, he dropped the tan box deliberately. He could almost feel his feet jarring the mines beneath them. If he stopped for one instant...

The ground under him began to buckle and roar. The silver sky tilted a little. Matt braced his feet as he ran, and took a long leap.

Explosion from the area outside the towers threw him up and forward. He crashed against a tree, slid down it while trying to put his arms around it, and lay with his face toward the ground while the whole planet of Set seemed to rock in its orbit and deafen his ears with its detonations.

Finally, the noise died. Matt got shakily to his feet and turned around. Time was watching the clearing. The ship was a useless tangled jumble. And no towers remained. The last ruins of the Pear Worshippers had fallen, and now they lay piled, stone on mighty stone, pressing down, covering over the fuel and the weapons of Marco Cain.

His brother would come back and find wreckage.

Time was chortling quietly. "Blew the damn place sky high...blew it sky high..."

Matt's eyes fastened on Arna. She stood straight, gazing back at him from the helmet someone had given her.

"Are you important to my brother?" he asked cynically.

"Certainly. So important that..."

His brother would come back and find...*nothing!*

"Mister Time," Matt said sharply.

The little man knocked the padded heels of his suit together. "Yessir," his voice came through the phone.

"Take this woman back to the *Caliban* and lock her in one of the food bins. Don't give her anything to eat or drink...for a while."

Time called up a detail and they marched Arna off through the silent forest where the birds still dipped and howled. She looked back once, the sleepy expression gone. Her whole body was tense, rigid, drawn in harsh lines.

"How much can one person hate somebody else?" she asked softly, her voice sounding tiny and edged through the phone.

"I know, I know," Matt laughed. "I'm still rotten." He put his lips around a cigarette, drew it from the container inside the helmet, lit it on a small grid. Puffing smoke, he let his anger rise in him. She and her detail were just vanishing through the foliage.

"Kick her." Matt said evenly. "In the stomach."

ONE OF THE men looked around, wondering, then he realized who had given the order and he brought up his knee and ground it into her middle. She doubled over. The guards dragged her on through the mud. The black filth spattered on her white legs. Matt heard her soft groaning in the com phones as she vanished from sight.

"Assemble, march formation back," Matt ordered.

The men swung into line, some of them mumbling about the order Matt had given. They didn't like to see a woman kicked, Matt knew, but this one belonged to Marco. It was almost like injuring Marco himself.

He called for the *Caliban* to drop her reflection screens. Stripping off his suit inside the lock, he returned with the mate to the chart room, watched the beam type.

This time, the message said that Marco and his men had burned a whole city on Panbal, destroying the families of three thousand Sol workers. There had been torture, too. Unpleasant, stomach-turning torture.

"That's just one more thing I'll pay him for," Matt whispered. "He'll build himself up, slaughter after slaughter and I'll knock him off and get a Tri-galactic for it."

"You hope you'll knock him off," Time said doubtfully.

"I wouldn't question my orders, if I were you," Matt said loudly so that all the astrogators could hear. "I wouldn't even question my opinions. You found that out once, didn't you?"

Time rubbed his metal-plated skull in exasperation. "For God's sake, Matt, cut it out. Stop acting like you're the biggest man space has ever seen. Marco feels that way, too. Sometime, one of the biggest men in space is going to have to die."

"It won't be me," Matt said, wondering deep down, if he was right. Marco was striking oftener, harder. Would the destruction of the supply dump make any difference? Fuel, one ship, and a handful of men...

...and Arna!"

"New orders," he barked. "Prepare to lift immediately."

Time relayed the orders.

"If I asked you," Matt said to the little man, "for the most God forsaken planet in the whole galaxy, the one farthest away from human life, what would you give me?"

"Ithar," Time replied without thought.

"The course is for Ithar."

Time gaped at him, but proceeded to carry out orders.

Exultantly, Matt went down to the great galley, moved among rows of hydroponic trays, rows of bright kettles hanging from racks. The Martian chief cook gave him a loaf of fresh warm bread.

In the storage hold, Matt unlocked one of the big doors to a food bin. It creaked and rattled open. Overhead lights in the high ceiling made a long bar of illumination in the bin.

Arna was crouched, naked and shivering, on a mound of potatoes. That seemed marvelously funny to Matt. He laughed, tossing her the bread and some self-lighting cigarettes.

"Cold?" he said wryly. "I hope not, because you're going to have a long ride. Maybe it'll warm you up!"

She cursed him, quietly, vengefully. To Matt's surprise, she then reached for his riot gun and grabbed it. Matt grabbed her arm and squeezed until the weapon fell to the floor. He shoved her backwards and she fell back onto the mound of potatoes. Matt picked up the weapon, slid the door shut, and locked it. It was funny. Arna, the beautiful naked woman, crouching on top of potatoes.

The jets began to roar.

It was tremendously funny. Matt rested his back against the locker door and laughed for a long, long time.

CHAPTER FOUR
The Frozen Hours

LIKE SOME huge silver slug, the *Caliban I* lay on the frozen tundra of Ithar. Behind the ship, mountains rose bleakly, swept by freezing winds. The plain of ice went away to the horizon, a deep shadowed black. Two moons, like round white snowballs, hung over the crags. The sky was a rich velvety blue, covered with stars. Snow whorls moved on the plain, misty dancers leaping up, falling back, leaping again with the voices of wind.

Matt stood outside Lock A, shrouded in a great fur parka. His cigarette made a spot of light in the somber landscape. When he exhaled, the wind caught the smoke and whipped it away across the wasteland.

Eighteen hours they had been on Ithar. Eighteen hours without a reply to the message that drummed out, at fifteen-minute intervals, across the galaxy. Where was Marco now? Sweeping down on the space lanes, plundering the ships, turning the crewmen out into the void? Where was his laugh echoing now, in some far-off street of a great city, where women screamed and were raped in the streets, where blood dripped from windowsills?

Marco strode across space in the thousand-league boots of teleportation, putting the torch to innumerable worlds. And, Matt thought, here I am, waiting for a reply to a stupid message. But it wasn't so stupid, really. Arna was out of the food locker now, considerably more quiet. She was in Time's cabin and Time was with the noncoms. Arna was a valuable property.

Matt entered the lock after throwing away his cigarette. As he passed through the inner portal and drew off the parka, he reflected that he had thought a great deal about Arna in the past few hours. Why, he couldn't say. Perhaps it was due to the fact that she was the only woman he had been near in—how many fierce, driving years? Oh, there had been women, but they had come and flared brightly for a while, an hour, two, and gone into the limbo of forgetfulness.

As he made his way to the bridge, he decided to have a talk with Arna. He was curious to find out more about her, where she came from, why she had taken up with Marco.

Marco…

That name, and the loathing it brought, drove her from his thoughts. In the chart room, a communications officer was busy at the beam type, clacking out the message on the machine Matt had had set up specially. He leaned over the officer's shoulder and watched the paper in fascination. It would be a lovely trap.

From Mt. Cain, Coordinates lane 44, subsector 2, point 0.859, PI Ithar. To Marco Cain, somewhere space. I've got Arna. You know that. I want to talk. Come if you want her back.

TIME'S VOICE interrupted his concentration. "Seems like we're always waiting for Marco, doesn't it."

"This will be the final wait," Matt replied.

"He might bring the fleet again."

"That doesn't worry me. When he goes to Set, he'll know I have her."

"He might think she was killed in the blast."

"He'll know I'm not lying. We've always been honest with one another…Matt's face darkened. "Up to now."

"You're fixing a trap for your brother?"

Matt faced Time, shaking a finger at him. "A trap that'll finish him. Without Marco, his men are helpless. And if I can get him alone, pretend to want to talk to him…I can kill him."

Time kept quiet for a minute. Then. "He'll have some men with him."

"But he won't be expecting me to cut him down where he stands. And that's exactly what I'll do."

"Tri-galactic means that much to you, does it?"

"Yes, it does."

"More than anything else?"

"Yes."

Time shook his head and smiled wanly. "May God have mercy on your soul," he said with gentle sarcasm.

"Hey!" the com officer shouted. "It's coming through!"

Matt pushed the officer out of the chair, sat down, his hands on the edge of the paper as it slid forth from the machine. He almost tore it loose as he got the message.

From Marco Cain, somewhere space. To my estimable brother. I'm coming to get her. And you'd better have all your ships there. You'll need them.

The machine went silent. Matt tore out the last of the paper, kept staring at it.

"There's more," Time said.

The machine clattered once again. The message was brief. *This is the big one, MC.*

Matt scrambled to his feet, knocking over the chair. "Let's go. We've got to collect some ships, like he said. After I kill him, we'll have to wipe up his fleet. Completely. That'll finish the job in the right way."

They took the elevator to the com room. Matt stood under the eighty-foot Galactic switchboard, mike in hand.

"All channels open?" he said to an officer.

The officer nodded.

"Attention all war rockets. Attention all war rockets in Galaxy Eighteen. This is Commander Cain. Five hundred of you will be designated to come to Ithar to furnish assistance. There is going to be a large combat force..."

He stopped. The officer in charge was fiddling with dials. The lights on the high board remained dark.

"What's wrong?" Matt asked. "We're sending, aren't we?"

"I think so, sir," the officer replied. But there are no receiving signals."

"You mean that the com machinery on everyone of our ships is out?"

"Either that sir, or..." The man flushed deeply, moving a switch back and forth.

"Or what? Damn you, speak up."

"He means," Time put in quietly, "either that, or there aren't any more of our ships left."

Matt choked. "W...w...what? Are you serious?"

TIME NODDED, metal skull glinting in the bright lights. "He could have done it. With teleportation, he could be all over the galaxy in the eighteen hours we've been here. Arriving one place, destroying three ships with a dozen or so of his own, teleporting to another sector, destroying more ships. We shouldn't have divided our strength."

"We had to. Otherwise, the cargo lanes would have been unprotected."

Time carefully lit a cigarette. The tension in the room mounted. "I'll wager that the cargo lanes are wide open now. The galaxy's like a trapped animal. There's no place to run any more. There's no protection anywhere."

Matt swore vengefully. He knotted his fist around the microphone and threw it against the board. It shattered and hung in a fan of silver chunks at the end of the long cord. The cord slid back into the wall. The pieces rattled when they struck the board.

"What would you suggest we do now?" Matt said, almost shouting.

"There's nothing to do now but wait for Marco. And his ships. If he decides to blow us to pieces with his vortex cannon, there's nothing we can do then, either. If he comes aboard and talks, you may get a chance to kill him. He might want the satisfaction of seeing you crawl, but we'd still have his whole fleet to buck. One war rocket against two hundred is pretty heavy odds."

"That's encouraging," Matt said nastily. "All right, so we wait."

He turned and walked out of the room. For a long time he wandered in the corridors of the ship, climbing up and down to the various decks, sitting on companion ladders with his cloak pulled around him, smoking and thinking.

Trapped, was all he could think. *Trapped and waiting for the butcher to come and slice us up in bloody little pieces.*

When he looked up finally, saw the thick carpeting on the floor and Time's door in front of him, he knew he had been heading there instinctively, all along.

He knocked hesitantly, although he had a key.

Arna opened the door. She was pushing the hair out of her eyes, and she looked sleepy once more. Surprise darted across her face, then wariness.

"What do you want?"

"Can I come in?" He leaned tiredly against the doorframe.

"What for?"

"I want to talk. I just want to sit down and talk."

She motioned him inside. The cabin was warm. Arna walked over to a divan, sat down, pulling the thick woolen bathrobe close around her. "Your first mate has very good liquor and very small clothes." The bathrobe barely covered her knees.

Matt grinned weakly, sat down across from her. He took a whisky bottle off the small cart and took a long drink. Fire started to run around in his stomach. It was pleasant fire. The lights in the room were soft purple, restful on the eyes. Arna leaned on the back of the divan, head on her arm, watching him.

"I *am* rotten," he said, taking another drink. "And tired, at that."

"Don't you like the frozen countryside?" she asked, smiling with mockery.

"I'm nuts about it. I'll be buried in it. We'll all be. Your lover took care of that."

She sat up straight, her eyes open wide. "Don't call him that."

"What?"

"My lover."

HE WAVED the bottle and took another drink, slouching down. He felt particularly nasty, but now he felt like being nasty to himself. "The man you go to bed with, then."

"That's it. That's all right. It was a business arrangement. I was working in a third-rate video studio on Rogweb in Galaxy Four. Your brother was there. A revolution was on. I met your brother. He was being paid to lead troops in the revolution. He told me a lot of things, how he would bleed Galaxy Eighteen, knock you down from your noble perch. It sounded very nice. I came along, like I always do, when there's something to be had."

The liquor began to thicken Matt's tongue. He unfastened his cloak and threw it on the floor. The red lining shimmered.

"Blood," he mumbled. "Mine. Yours. Everybody's. Except Marco's."

"You ought to talk sense."

"It isn't sensible," he replied roughly. He kept on talking, spilling out the situation. She listened. When he was finished, he took another drink from the bottle. It was empty. He reached for a second.

"So you're going to kill him if he comes to see you."

"He'd kill me," Matt replied defensively.

"Does that make it right?"

"Oh, sentimental," he said sarcastically. "Very sentimental. Now you're dead and in your grave and you want me to shower him with brotherly love. Listen... He struggled over the word. Saliva filled his mouth. He swallowed.

"Listen," he began again. "It's been going on since we were kids, back in the Ganymede Outlands, Galaxy One. Get ahead. Get ahead of the other one. Marco's got a girl. Matt has to get a girl. Marco gets a prettier one. Marco gets money. It goes on and on and on." He drank again.

"You've always been running just a little behind him?"

"Yes, just a little. He enjoys watching me lag. He's always got to be ahead. That's why we hate each other, I guess."

"Have you ever killed anyone before. I mean, the way you're going to kill Marco?"

He pursed his lips and peered at her. The room had a film around the edge, but she was in the center, very clear. "No."

"Has he?"

"Killed anyone? Oh sure, three or four that I know of. Always got to be ahead, you know."

"I hope you don't kill him, Matt."

He gurgled drunkenly. "That's pretty. Say my name again. It's pretty."

She paid no attention, hurried on softly, insistently. "Don't kill him. People like us can do a lot of rotten things, but once we take that last step, killing someone without being attacked, we can't ever go back to being even halfway decent and clean inside."

He stood up, swaying. The bottle was raised. "Lovely talk," he said loudly. "We're all so decent, all of us in this stinking pigpen." He spit out the last words. Drops of saliva sailed through the beam of a lamp, burned, vanished.

His legs went rubbery under him. The bottle rolled on the floor, dripping liquor on the rug. Matt struggled on his knees. He fell forward onto the rug, one hand twitching. He whimpered, "We're all so damned decent..."

She was pulling at him then. Pulling him up to a sitting position. Her face was close to his, the hair falling down, touching his face with a warm tingling. "We can try to be, Matt."

Helping him to his feet, she stood close to him. The purple lights moved in her hair. Like he was reaching out to touch some strange object, he put his arms around her, wonderingly. She held him tightly, her mouth searching his.

He was lost between worlds, wandering out where there was no Marco, no frozen tundras of ice, no death and no drive. For a moment, he was lost in purple and breaking rainbows and shards of sunlight and all the old songs he had always wanted to listen to and enjoy.

And then he was back in Time's cabin, with a desirable woman in his arms. The brain fog seemed to clear a little bit. He put his left arm under her legs, lifted her. She lay against his shoulder, kissing his neck.

He took one step.

"Do...do you want it...this way... like this..." he mumbled.

"Yes," she said, over and over.

He walked on and on, through fields of night. Something got in his way. He kicked it aside. For dark joyous miles he walked, and then at last he did not have to walk any more.

He found the strange world again, below heaven, above hell, where there were only sunlit mornings and music and warm arms drawing him down and down and down forever...

THUNDER, beating and beating in his brain. Slowly and slowly diminishing, until it was only a fist, pounding on the door. Matt staggered into the main room, tucking in his shirt. He pulled the door open, stuck his neck forward, finally saw Time.

The little man was rubbing his metal hand into his other palm, excitedly. "Message coming through," he blurted, "from your brother."

Arna called to him from the darkness. "Marco," he yelled, scooping up his cloak and slamming the door. They ran toward the elevator. Matt bumped unsteadily against the wall, but kept on going.

"Is he coming?" Matt cried anxiously.

"Don't know," Time told him as the elevator began to hum downward. "The message just began to come through. I couldn't raise you on the com anywhere in the ship. I took a chance on her."

They walked rapidly into the chart room. Nearly all of the fuzziness was gone from his brain. He felt instead, a cool relief. He was ready for whatever might be coming.

The com officer at the special beam type handed him the paper.

To Matthew Cain, From Marco Cain. Thanks for waiting, brother. It gave me time to assemble my fleet. You have no more ships, you know, except the flagship. I'm going to take the Galaxy apart piece by piece, and then hunt you down. First stop, Merthor.

Time nodded. "He knows he's got us. There are...good God eighteen million people on Merthor and the repair shops...and the factories...almost all of the Sol resources that are left. If he gets Merthor, he's finished Galaxy Eighteen. And he won't stop there."

"Merthor," Matt whispered.

The room was silent. Beyond the high catwalk and the great observation window, wind ghosts cavorted on the plain. The snowball moons rose upward in the sky over Ithar.

"If we wait here," Matt reasoned aloud, "we're finished. Correct?"

Time nodded again.

"We're dead men, Time. Dead men on a dead ship. Marco's heading for Merthor with a fleet of say, two hundred. He can teleport all the way around the planet in a moment, correct?"

The steel head waggled again. Matt laughed.

"Then tell me this," Matt breathed. "How much damage can a ship full of dead men do?"

Time thought. He flexed his left hand. The metal joints squeaked faintly.

"They should," he said slowly, "be able to do a lot. If they're dead, they haven't got much to lose."

Matt roared with triumphant laughter. "I've got one hell of a smart first officer." His hand seized the microphone. He yelled orders. "Stations. Raise ship immediately. Course for Merthor. Full power. Get off your big fat tails and get to work!"

The old fire was racing through him, consuming him, but it was tempered with new strength. Strength that made unbreakable chains out of soft hair, strength that made powerful drugs from a half-awake expression.

THE jets exploded. The astrogators whipped out fresh charts, began plotting coordinates. Matt vaulted up the ladder to the catwalk, watched Ithar with its mountains and its icefall away under them. Then the atmosphere was gone, and the galaxy stretched wide and waiting, for the iron colossus with the heart of atomic burning. The *Caliban I* vibrated and plunged through the dark.

Time joined him.

Matt clapped him on the back. "A coffin ship full of corpses, eh, Time? But we'll make the biggest damned funeral pyre Galaxy Eighteen ever saw. Looks like there's no Tri-galactic in the offing."

"Looks that way," Time agreed.

"Just a chance to finish a few of Marco's friends."

"What about Marco himself?"

Matt shook his black tangled head slowly. "I don't think we'll get that far."

The *Caliban* rushed on, bleeding a trail to slash the blackness. Merthor began to grow, a planet two worlds away from a huge yellow sun.

"Twelve thousand miles off," Time reported, coming on the catwalk. "Correct to schedule, correct to course."

"We'll be..."

The *Caliban* lurched. Matt leaped for the window. The galaxy seemed to be falling away, or perhaps the ship seemed to be falling down into a spatial well. The stars went upward and the inside of the ship grew deathly cold.

Matt screamed frantically, *"Counter-warp drive!"*

Someone relayed the order. A whining hum rose in the bowels of the ship. Gradually, they seemed to pull up out of the funnel of infinite black. The coldness seeped away. The plates stopped their protesting groans. Once more they were thundering toward Merthor.

Matt leaned against the wall, rubbing his forehead. "I'd almost forgotten that was there. Another moment and we'd have been through the warp and dead and frozen in hyper-space."

"And no way to get back," Time put in. "No way for the coffin ship to get back and fight."

The hour ticked slowly away. Matt watched as the *Caliban* swirled into the misty upper atmosphere of the planet.

"Look down there," he pointed. A city was blazing, a great bonfire of ships and humanity and machines. The day side of the planet was a smoking ruin.

"The night side," Matt breathed. "That's where he is." He raised his voice, felt the hoarseness in it. *"Alter course!"*

Time dictated the new coordinates. The *Caliban* flashed around Merthor, crossed the dark unreal line of twilight, plunged into the darkness. More cities were burning. The face of the world was exploding. Tiny dots of ships appeared, vanished, appeared again, outlined in the glow of the holocaust.

"Greb," Matt said. "The main base...it's still untouched."

"They must be saving it for the last."

"We're going down."

The *Caliban* reared and nosed downward. Matt clambered off the catwalk, picked up the phone.

"Cannoneers!" he shouted, his voice huge and joyous and mad. *"Stations!"*

He turned to Time, shook the little man's hand. "Watch out for Arna. I'll see you sometime."

Time's eyes got distant, faintly dim. He swallowed, hard, pressed Matt's hand. "Sure, Matt, sometime."

"I'm going up with the guns," Matt called, stripping off his cloak and tunic as he ran.

In the forward gunroom, the air was hot and heavy, like a humid blue dusk. The cannoneers grunted and adjusted their coordinates, their bodies shining with sweat in the small pilot lights.

Matt raced into the room, shouted to them.

"Guns ready," one of them reported.

53

"Let me do this," Matt breathed, climbing up into the high seat. He strapped himself down, put his hands on the control lever. He sighted through the view tube.

Below, a part of the city of Greb was beginning to burn. A ship marked with a phosphorous *MC* flashed before the view tube. Matt yanked the lever.

The ship rocked, and the vortex spread out and enveloped the other ship. It vanished in a cloud of thundering whiteness.

Like some fantastic god, dripping with sweat, Matt rocked in the firing seat, pulling the lever and laughing, while the *Caliban I* plunged deeper into the fury, deeper into the battle that was already lost.

CHAPTER FIVE
The Coffin Ship

FOR seemingly endless hours, the *Caliban* dipped and bucked over the city of Greb. Blasts shook the hull. The vortex cannons spewed out their white force. Marco's ships vanished entirely or flamed scarlet in the dark, or dropped, great pieces shearing away, bodies tumbling out of the wrecked ships to bloat tremendously and splatter a rain of blood and soft gray guts over space.

Matt pulled the cannon-firing lever, pulled it again, again. His muscles contorted like snakes under his sweating hide. His laughter went on, rising, now falling, vanishing to a macabre chuckle, fountaining up to a tremendous rocking peak.

One of the crewmen was pulling at his arm, frantically thrusting forward a microphone and a receiver with the other hand. Matt jerked the lever once more, squinting through the eye tube. The vortex flashed, encircling one of Matt's ships. It ceased to exist.

"Urgent message from the bridge, sir," the cannoneer barked.

Matt paused for a moment, seemed to collect his thoughts. Then he unstrapped himself, got down wearily from the high seat. He gestured to another of the cannoneers.

"Take over."

Eagerly, a slaty Venusian scrambled up.

Matt put the phone to his ear. "This is Cain," he said rapidly.

"Time, Matt. They're beginning to notice us. We've been dropping quite a few of their tin cans."

"I think you'd better come up to the bridge."

"Why?"

"The fleet is pulling out into space, collecting itself. They're corning to get us, all at once."

"How many?"

"Oh, maybe a hundred and fifty."

"Is the flagship still up?" Matt's voice was soft, anxious, vicious.

"I can't be sure."

Matt dropped the phone, ran toward the door. The gunroom was filled with an acrid smoky haze. The pilot lights gleamed and danced along the wet bodies of the men.

In the elevator, Matt leaned weakly against the wall, gasping air into his tortured lungs. It wouldn't be very long before they were finished. But meanwhile...

The elevator stopped. Matt walked into the chart room. Arna was there, with Time. She was awake now, dressed in a regulation tunic and breeches. She stood with feet wide apart, watching him, a strange kind of brilliance lighting up her eyes. Her breasts thrust against the tunic, moving up down, up down, quickly.

Matt squeezed her hand, felt the fingers warm on his. To Time he said, "You kept the ship moving well. We accounted for quite a few."

"I'd advise you to go up there and look for yourself," Time said worriedly.

"All right. Meanwhile, get me the commander down at Greb."

He vaulted up the ladder to the catwalk. Far out in space, beyond the night side of the planet, ships were gathering, outlined in the fiery glare from the cities that burned on the other side of Merthor. Faint splotches of light were on those ships. Matt knew those splotches were letters.

"We haven't got long," he said, agreeing with Time when he came down from the window. Time handed him the phone, saying, "Greb."

"Hello," Matt said sharply. "This is Commander Cain."

A VOICE, bearing heavy guttural traces, said, "Von Feist, Captain of Transport Base."

"How badly is the city hit?"

"Not too badly, *Herr Cain*. Some of the outer buildings are burning. Only a few of the vortex blasts landed."

"Have you got any ships?"

"*Ach... nein, Herr Cain,* only a few cargo transports, light classes mostly, thirty or so fliers...nothing heavy with armament..."

"Put them up," Matt ordered. "Have you got enough men to handle them?" He wiped a trickle of sweat running down his chest.

"With skeleton crews, yes, but of what possible use..."

"Damn you," Matt yelled. "I said put them up. Right away. You've got women and kids in the city, haven't you?"

"Yes, oh yes, *Herr Cain*. My family..."

"Then put up those ships."

The voice became precise. "Very well, *Herr Cain*. Any further orders?"

"Yes. There's one way to do damage to enemy ships."

Silence crackled audibly over the connection. Arna held tightly to Matt's hand. At last, Von Feist replied, "Certainly, *Herr Cain*. One way. *Ram them.*"

Matt waved, almost as if he thought Von Feist could see. "Ram them, crash them, bust up their jets— I don't care what happens, just as long as we get them out of the sky."

Von Feist began to talk excitedly. *"Ja, Herr Cain... Ja...ich werde..."*

Matt slammed down the receiver. Time was up on the catwalk. He leaned over the railing, his face pale.

He said, "Here they come."

Matt grinned, put his arms around Arna, kissing her hard. He was afraid, his stomach was a great yawning void, but he had to show them that they could still fight. Releasing Arna, he shouted with a defiance he didn't feel, "Let them come! We've got more coffins on the way!"

Ragged cheering broke out, spattered on the walls, died.

Matt dialed the central com room. "Get me my brother's flagship." He put down the phone, lit a cigarette and waited.

He jerked around when the buzzer sounded. His hand fastened on the phone, scooping it up. A voice said, "Proceed."

"Well?" It was Marco's voice.

Matt breathed deeply. "Let's finish this, brother."

"The two of us?"

"Yes." Matt laughed jaggedly. "Just the two of us."

"I can blast you out of the sky. We're coming down on you right now."

"Are you full of fear, brother?" Matt's voice bit and tore. "Are you afraid you can't get ahead of your puny relative?"

There was a long silence. And then Marco began to curse, the words tumbling one upon another, filthy, obscene. At last he said quietly, *"Where?"*

Matt thought briefly. "Around on the other side, out in space. Do you know where the warp is?"

"Yes."

"Bring your flagship. I'll bring the *Caliban*. We'll draw along side. Put on a suit and meet me on top of the ship. No firing until…one of us comes back. Agreed?"

"Agreed, you son of—"

"Mutual," Matt whispered and put the phone in its cradle.

"Prepare to accelerate," he called.

"New course. Draw up just outside the attraction field of the warp. I'm going to the upper lock."

Time followed, with Arna. Matt wondered how the other ships were faring. Now it didn't matter. All that mattered was Marco.

IN THE UPPER lock chamber, Matt pulled on his suit. Arna lit a cigarette for him, put it between his lips. The jets stopped coughing. The *Caliban* was silent.

"We're at the warp," Time announced dismally. "What weapons?"

"Just give me a knife."

Time offered his. The blade shone. Matt stuffed it into the voluminous belt. The lights in the ceiling made yellow cones on the floor. Matt stood outside one of the cones, holding his helmet crooked in one arm, blowing smoke into the column of light and watching it twist up and around. Time's left hand was a dull gleam in the darkness. Arna leaned on his shoulder.

"Friends, Romans and corpses," Matt said suddenly in a loud voice. "The dead man's final speech to his..." He choked. He rubbed his eyes. He lowered his head and said very faintly, "God."

"How will we know what happens?" Time asked, from somewhere in the dark.

"The ships'll be hull to hull," Matt breathed. "Whichever one of us...stays alive...will get back to his ship and order the vortex cannons fired. The other ship...just won't be."

"I see," Time murmured.

There was a soft gentle chunking against the hull.

"Here he is," Time said.

"Well," said Matt with a long sigh. Hurriedly Arna put her arms around his neck, her lips close to his ear. "Come back, Matt. Remember there's something to come back for."

Matt flipped away his cigarette. It lay in the cone of yellow, still burning. He said, "Marco's got something to come back for, too. Power. That's a lot to come back for."

She pulled away. "Haven't you got anything more?"

He looked at her for a long minute, feeling for the first time in many years that the toughness, the hardness, was gone, and that he was only a child, alone somewhere in a mournful graveyard where the wind twisted the leaves around the tombstones under the swollen moon.

He said, "I wish I knew," and jammed the helmet onto his head, snapping the locks closed. Without looking at either of them, he felt forward. He fumbled for the switch, the ladder rungs, pulled himself up—crawled up into the tiny escape chamber, lay there shivering in the dark while the air whispered away.

The upper door *spanged* open.

Reluctantly he put his gloved hands on the edge of the opening and lifted. Getting to his feet, he looked around.

The burnished hull of the *Caliban I* stretched downward on each side of him. To his right, flush against his own craft, lay Marco's flagship. The stars were cold eyes, and the day side of Merthor was blackened with smoke and destruction.

To his left lay the warp, an almost tangible circle of blacker black, a hole out of the universe, a gateway to the broken dimensions.

Marco was nowhere to be seen on top of his own ship.

When the attack came, it came suddenly.

A KIND OF animal snarl came through Matt's headphone. He felt an arm holding him from behind slipping around his neck, binding him with horrible strength. There was a ripping sound.

There was a very quiet hiss.

The arm let go. Matt turned around, staring dumbly. Behind Marco's helmet, he could see eyes full of the wolf-luster of hate. Marco waved his knife. The air kept hissing out of Matt's suit.

"You've got fifteen seconds to live," Marco said.

And Matt whispered, *"...from behind..."*

And Marco laughed.

The air made a roar, like ocean surf at dawn, vanishing and leaving. His body would explode...dead man...

Marco kept on laughing. *Matt, the dead man...*

And then he thought of Arna.

He saw her, quite clearly, in his mind. He started to walk forward. Marco didn't laugh any more. A horrible burning pain ran along Matt's arms. He knew that it was a dead man's final flow of strength.

He took hold of his brother's suit. Marco whimpered crazily, drove his knife forward. It ripped into the suit, made a probe of torture in his side. Marco pulled it all the way out.

He was conscious of a strangeness in his body, as if his soul were chained up and had to be released. It cried and groaned and twisted inside of him. He knew it was only the pressure, the pressure that would blow him into a thousand soggy pieces of bone and blood...

Marco stabbed him in the side a second time. Matt picked him up, with that terrible strength pouring through him. *Arna,* his brain sang, *Arna Arna Arna...*

He held Marco over his head. Marco screamed.

He threw him, outward and forward. Marco clawed the dark air. There was nothing to stop him. Nothing...

And the warp was waiting.

His body fell into that blackness, and seemed to become some insane jigsaw puzzle, with angular planes, Marco torn apart and put back together as a hundred different beings in that empty hole where there were no laws of matter.

And then he was gone and only the warp remained. There was the scream, bouncing back from endless tangential walls of twisted dimensions, and then that, too, vanished.

Matt dropped the knife, heard it clank and slide away. He took a step. His body was expanding, getting monstrously heavy. There was only a faint hiss of air now.

He tried to take another step. The lock was an open square, a few feet away. Another step...

Arna...

He screamed her name. *"Arna...Arna...Arna..."*

Somehow, he pushed across the infinite distances and fell down into the lock in a tortured heap. He heard the door clanging automatically closed, the air beginning to return. His body seemed to contract.

There was metallic coldness under him. He jerked off the helmet, breathing the thin air, pressing his face against that coldness.

There was blood inside his suit. It was warm. It was rising.

It was an invisible, sweeping up over his chest, his shoulders, in the dark. He lay, murmuring her name a thousand times until the warm tide closed over his head and he was drowned.

"HE CAME from behind me," Matt kept repeating.

The Healing Plasters covered the wounds in his side, white plastic strips that would cleanse and repair the ragged cuts made by Marco's knife. He shook his head in a dazed fashion, saw that he was in his cabin, and breathed deeply of the air.

"How long have I been out?" he asked weakly.

"About an hour," Time told him.

Arna's hand moved along his cheek, warm possessive. He touched her fingers, trying to smile.

"He came at me from behind," he said again.

"You told us," Arna said. "You babbled the whole story while we got you down from the airlock."

"Where's his flagship?"

"Still beside us," Time said. "Still waiting for one of you to come back."

Matt struggled to his feet. "Don't..." Arna began. He shoved her hand away roughly.

"There's still a little work to do. Time, is there anybody aboard who can operate a teleporter?"

Time pondered, finally said, "I'm not sure. I'll check." He took the com phone from a small alcove in the wall, talked quietly for a few moments, then turned around.

"A breed Martian in the galley. Used to be with Morgan's men in Galaxy Six. The Invisible ships...you remember..."

Matt nodded. "Get him up here. Assemble all the men in the locks, fully armed."

Time frowned. "Why?"

"We're taking over Marco's flagship."

Matt stumbled to a closet, selected a cloak and threw it around him.

"Too much strain on the Plasters and they'll break," Arna warned.

Matt kissed her quickly. "Then just pray that they don't break for another half-chron." He swung around and the cloak flapped from his shoulders. "All right, Time, let's go."

The men were crowded in the locks. Matt spoke brief orders into the com phones and the doors of the *Caliban I* opened to reveal other doors. The torch crews began slicing through the metal with silent white beams of heat.

Matt, sword in one hand, blaster gripped in the other, tried to stop the hammers of pain ringing in his skull. But they clanged and beat and echoed like a thousand broken bells.

The doors of Marco's flagship dissolved. Matt swept his blade in the air, and his men plunged into the ship.

They started on the lower decks, with the advantage of surprise. They swept down the metal halls, up the ladders. They opened every door, killed every crewman they found. Little rivers of blood began to run in the passageways.

The engine room...the galley...the arms room...silently they ticked off the conquered sectors. They stalked quietly, killed quietly, a great tide of steel and hatred that swept upward and outward through the iron guts of the ship. Matt was there, and Time, vengefully slaying...and slaying...and slaying...

THEY BATTERED down the doors of the chart room. In the center, on a round platform, stood the gigantic bulk of the teleportation unit. A few technicians fired blasters from a balcony. Matt's men spread out and began to pick them off, one by one. Bodies tumbled lazily to the floor, bones snapping with finality.

The room reeked of blaster smell. Matt breathed deeply, Time at his side. The last of the defenders was gone.

And then, from behind a pillar on the catwalk, a blue Mercurial with one arm reared up, half of the other shoulder gone. But his blaster went forward and a beam of force sizzled out.

Time screamed. The metal plate in his skull turned molten. He screamed louder, pulling at the top of his head, trying to quench the tide of fiery dripping hell that ran down his face, burned out his eyes, charred his skin away. He skittered along the floor, bumped against an astrogation table and lay still.

Blasters came up all around the room. The Mercurial, teetering on the edge of the catwalk, aimed at Matt.

Face like a mask of stone, Matt flung his sword. It arched like a shimmering fish through the air and skewered the Mercurial's stomach. He dropped, sagging across the railing with the blade sticking out at the base of his spine, covered with blue ooze.

Matt leaned on one of the tables. His strength was draining away. But he had to stay up...for a little while longer...he prayed to strange blasphemous gods that the Plasters would not break.

The breed Martian, obsequious and servile, reported.

"Stand by the machinery," Matt said in a deathly whisper. "Orbeck. Somebody get me Orbeck."

The beefy man pushed through the crowd. "Here, sir."

"Take the ship around to the other side of Merthor." Matt sank down onto a stool, looking deep into the red haze before his eyes, as the chemical drive boomed.

Eons later, Orbeck said, "We're twelve miles off."

"Any of Marco's ships still up?"

"About sixty, sir."

Matt nodded. "The suicide crew did their job. Get the coordinates of that warp on the other side."

Orbeck returned from the file in a few minutes. "Now," said Matt, "have that Martian rig the arrival end of the teleporter just inside the field of attraction of the warp."

Again Orbeck went, seemingly through far oceans of dim wavering redness. Again his fat face thrust through the murk. "Done, sir."

"Give me the com phone. Get all those other ships on the hookup."

Someone put the phone into his hand. Matt wondered if he could talk any more.

"You may go ahead, sir," Orbeck whispered.

"This is Cain," Matt said, trying to approximate his brother's voice. "I'm wounded. Assemble before the flagship immediately."

At the observation port, someone yelled, "They're leaving Greb. They're coming this way."

"How is the city?" Matt wondered. He tried to look at his hand, could not find it in that awful red sea.

"Only about a quarter burned," the voice called back.

There were small noises in the redness. Men coughing. The hum of the teleport generators gathering power. Orbeck talking to someone about Matt. He smiled at that or, at least, smiled inside of himself. He could barely move.

Orbeck said at last, after infinities, "They're drawn up before us. All of them."

"Teleport them," Matt whispered. *Into the warp.*

A BANSHEE whine ran through the ship, like a woman crying out with her mouth wide open. It keened up and up, and abruptly broke off.

"They're gone," Orbeck breathed, returning. "Every last one of them. Gone."

Matt felt relief run through his veins like warm liquor. "Let me see," he whispered. "Lead me to the catwalk..."

"I really don't think you should, sir," Orbeck replied. "The Plasters seem strained...the fibers are full of small cracks."

"Take me to where I can see," Matt said.

Orbeck half lifted, half pushed him up the ladder toward the catwalk. Near the top, Matt threw off his hands, head back, infinitely proud and sick.

"I'll...go...up...alo..."

Someone yelled. Orbeck dodged instinctively. Matt's legs went out from under him. He fell down the ladder and lay on the floor. The Healing Plasters split and the wounds began to bleed again, soaking the white plastic fibers with sticky redness.

"Hurry," Orbeck howled, beefy face flushed. "Get him below. Ship's medic…hurry…"

CHAPTER SIX
The Final Honor

THE SKY was a very bright blue, filled with little puffs of white cloud. Beyond the base, the hills rose, green and shimmering in the wind.

Long lines of men in dress uniform stood at attention all the way down the field. From somewhere rolled the steady beat of kettledrums.

In the center of the field, the High Commander of *Sol, Incorporated* nodded to an orderly.

"Captain Vincent Orbeck," the orderly announced. The drums thundered.

Orbeck walked stiffly forward, conscious of his own bulk. His boots drummed on the concrete. He tried to march in time to the drums.

He stopped before the High Commander, feeling awe under the stern gaze, the face like worn leather. The High Commander's scarlet plume danced fitfully in the wind.

The High Commander casually extended his hand. Orbeck shook it.

"To Galactic Commander Matthew Cain," the orderly read, "is awarded the honorary post of Tri-galactic commander."

He handed a small velvet box to Orbeck. The stern gaze relaxed for a minute. Orbeck watched the sky, squinting.

"Tell me, Captain Orbeck," said the High Commander, "why would a man like Matthew Cain do a thing like that?"

"I don't know, sir," Orbeck replied, knowing all along, wishing, somehow, that he could have done the same thing himself.

"Do you know where he is now?"

Orbeck lifted his eyes to the blue sky and the wind. "Out there. Out there with her. Wherever there's quiet, and perhaps books and wine and no more killing. Just the two of them."

The High Commander smiled rather thinly and spoke so softly that none of his aides could hear. "Sometimes I think that men like us don't really know what it is that we want, with our cannons and our ships and our desire for more worlds." The smile grew wry. "But then I guess that's why we're here."

"Yes, sir," Orbeck replied, catching himself a moment later and growing red all over his fleshy face.

"Well," the High Commander said reflectively, "I wish them both the best of luck. And if you ever see him again, give him the medal, will you?" The Commander indicated the box.

"Yes, sir, I will."

The High Commander stiffened. Orbeck knocked his boots together, faced about smartly and walked back toward the ranks of men. The drums beat. The sky was warm and blue and the wind moved in the green trees beyond the buildings.

Orbeck walked on, away from the High Commander, the box clutched tightly in his hand. He wished terribly that he could run, tear off his tunic, run away, find a woman like Matt had found one, and live forever in the stars with a final end to hunting. But then, he was an officer in Sol, Incorporated.

Next in line for Commander of Galaxy Eighteen.

He took up his place in line, about-faced. His fingers constricted around the box. Tri-galactic. That might be something else to work for. Not like the woman, the lovely woman...but something...

He stood among the ranks of men stretching down the concrete.

The kettledrums beat...

THE END

If you've enjoyed this book, you will not want to miss these terrific titles...

ARMCHAIR SCI-FI, FANTASY, & HORROR DOUBLE NOVELS, $12.95 each

D-1 **THE GALAXY RAIDERS** by William P. McGivern
SPACE STATION #1 by Frank Belknap Long

D-2 **THE PROGRAMMED PEOPLE** by Jack Sharkey
SLAVES OF THE CRYSTAL BRAIN by William Carter Sawtelle

D-3 **YOU'RE ALL ALONE** by Fritz Leiber
THE LIQUID MAN by Bernard C. Gilford

D-4 **CITADEL OF THE STAR LORDS** by Edmund Hamilton
VOYAGE TO ETERNITY by Milton Lesser

D-5 **IRON MEN OF VENUS** by Don Wilcox
THE MAN WITH ABSOLUTE MOTION by Noel Loomis

D-6 **WHO SOWS THE WIND...** by Rog Phillips
THE PUZZLE PLANET by Robert A. W. Lowndes

D-7 **PLANET OF DREAD** by Murray Leinster
TWICE UPON A TIME by Charles L. Fontenay

D-8 **THE TERROR OUT OF SPACE** by Dwight V. Swain
QUEST OF THE GOLDEN APE by Ivar Jorgensen and Adam Chase

D-9 **SECRET OF MARRACOTT DEEP** by Henry Slesar
PAWN OF THE BLACK FLEET by Mark Clifton.

D-10 **BEYOND THE RINGS OF SATURN** by Robert Moore Williams
A MAN OBSESSED by Alan E. Nourse

ARMCHAIR SCIENCE FICTION CLASSICS, $12.95 each

C-1 **THE GREEN MAN**
by Harold M. Sherman

C-2 **A TRACE OF MEMORY**
By Keith Laumer

C-3 **INTO PLUTONIAN DEPTHS**
by Stanton A. Coblentz

ARMCHAIR MASTERS OF SCIENCE FICTION SERIES, $16.95 each

M-1 **MASTERS OF SCIENCE FICTION, Vol. One**
Bryce Walton—"Dark of the Moon" and other tales

M-2 **MASTERS OF SCIENCE FICTION, Vol. Two**
Jerome Bixby—"One Way Street" and other tales

If you've enjoyed this book, you will not want to miss these terrific titles…

ARMCHAIR SCI-FI & HORROR DOUBLE NOVELS, $12.95 each

D-11   **PERIL OF THE STARMEN** by Kris Neville
        THE STRANGE INVASION by Murray Leinster

D-12   **THE STAR LORD** by Boyd Ellanby
        CAPTIVES OF THE FLAME by Samuel R. Delany

D-13   **MEN OF THE MORNING STAR** by Edmund Hamilton
        PLANET FOR PLUNDER by Hal Clement and Sam Merwin, Jr.

D-14   **ICE CITY OF THE GORGON** by Chester S. Geier and Richard Shaver
        WHEN THE WORLD TOTTERED by Lester Del Rey

D-15   **WORLDS WITHOUT END** by Clifford D. Simak
        THE LAVENDER VINE OF DEATH by Don Wilcox

D-16   **SHADOW ON THE MOON** by Joe Gibson
        ARMAGEDDON EARTH by Geoff St. Reynard

D-17   **THE GIRL WHO LOVED DEATH** by Paul W. Fairman
        SLAVE PLANET by Laurence M. Janifer

D-18   **SECOND CHANCE** by J. F. Bone
        MISSION TO A DISTANT STAR by Frank Belknap Long

D-19   **THE SYNDIC** by C. M. Kornbluth
        FLIGHT TO FOREVER by Poul Anderson

D-20   **SOMEWHERE I'LL FIND YOU** by Milton Lesser
        THE TIME ARMADA by Fox B. Holden

ARMCHAIR SCIENCE FICTION CLASSICS, $12.95 each

C-4   **CORPUS EARTHLING**
        by Louis Charbonneau

C-5   **THE TIME DISSOLVER**
        by Jerry Sohl

C-6   **WEST OF THE SUN**
        by Edgar Pangborn

ARMCHAIR SCIENCE FICTION & HORROR GEMS SERIES, $12.95 each

G-1   **SCIENCE FICTION GEMS, Vol. One**
        Isaac Asimov and others

G-2   **HORROR GEMS, Vol. One**
        Carl Jacobi and others

If you've enjoyed this book, you will not want to miss these terrific titles…

ARMCHAIR SCI-FI, FANTASY, & HORROR DOUBLE NOVELS, $12.95 each

D-21 **EMPIRE OF EVIL** by Robert Arnette
THE SIGN OF THE TIGER by Alan E. Nourse & J. A. Meyer

D-22 **OPERATION SQUARE PEG** by Frank Belknap Long
ENCHANTRESS OF VENUS by Leigh Brackett

D-23 **THE LIFE WATCH** by Lester Del Rey
CREATURES OF THE ABYSS by Murray Leinster

D-24 **LEGION OF LAZARUS** by Edmond Hamilton
STAR HUNTER by Andre Norton

D-25 **EMPIRE OF WOMEN** by John Fletcher
ONE OF OUR CITIES IS MISSING by Irving Cox

D-26 **THE WRONG SIDE OF PARADISE** by Raymond F. Jones
THE INVOLUNTARY IMMORTALS by Rog Phillips

D-27 **EARTH QUARTER** by Damon Knight
ENVOY TO NEW WORLDS by Keith Laumer

D-28 **SLAVES TO THE METAL HORDE** by Milton Lesser
HUNTERS OUT OF TIME by Joseph E. Kelleam

D-29 **RX JUPITER SAVE US** by Ward Moore
BEWARE THE USURPERS by Geoff St. Reynard

D-30 **SECRET OF THE SERPENT** by Don Wilcox
CRUSADE ACROSS THE VOID by Dwight V. Swain

ARMCHAIR SCIENCE FICTION CLASSICS, $12.95 each

C-7 **THE SHAVER MYSTERY, Book One**
by Richard S. Shaver

C-8 **THE SHAVER MYSTERY, Book Two**
by Richard S. Shaver

C-9 **MURDER IN SPACE** by David V. Reed
by David V. Reed

ARMCHAIR MASTERS OF SCIENCE FICTION SERIES, $16.95 each

M-3 **MASTERS OF SCIENCE FICTION, Vol. Three**
Robert Sheckley, "The Perfect Woman" and other tales

M-4 **MASTERS OF SCIENCE FICTION, Vol. Four**
Mack Reynolds, "Stowaway" and other tales

If you've enjoyed this book, you will not want to miss these terrific titles...

ARMCHAIR SCI-FI & HORROR DOUBLE NOVELS, $12.95 each

If you've enjoyed this book, you will not want to miss these terrific titles…

ARMCHAIR SCI-FI & HORROR DOUBLE NOVELS, $12.95 each

D-51   **A GOD NAMED SMITH** by Henry Slesar
        WORLDS OF THE IMPERIUM by Keith Laumer

D-52   **CRAIG'S BOOK** by Don Wilcox
        EDGE OF THE KNIFE by H. Beam Piper

D-53   **THE SHINING CITY** by Rena M. Vale
        THE RED PLANET by Russ Winterbotham

D-54   **THE MAN WHO LIVED TWICE** by Rog Phillips
        VALLEY OF THE CROEN by Lee Tarbell

D-55   **OPERATION DISASTER** by Milton Lesser
        LAND OF THE DAMNED by Berkeley Livingston

D-56   **CAPTIVE OF THE CENTAURIANESS** by Poul Anderson
        A PRINCESS OF MARS by Edgar Rice Burroughs

D-57   **THE NON-STATISTICAL MAN** by Raymond F. Jones
        MISSION FROM MARS by Rick Conroy

D-58   **INTRUDERS FROM THE STARS** by Ross Rocklynne
        FLIGHT OF THE STARLING by Chester S. Geier

D-59   **COSMIC SABOTEUR** by Frank M. Robinson
        LOOK TO THE STARS by Willard Hawkins

D-60   **THE MOON IS HELL!** by John W. Campbell, Jr.
        THE GREEN WORLD by Hal Clement

ARMCHAIR SCIENCE FICTION CLASSICS, $12.95 each

C-16   **THE SHAVER MYSTERY, Book Three**
        by Richard S. Shaver

C-17   **THE PLANET STRAPPERS**
        by Raymond Z. Gallun

C-18   **THE FOURTH "R"**
        by George O. Smith

ARMCHAIR SCIENCE FICTION & HORROR GEMS SERIES, $12.95 each

G-5   **SCIENCE FICTION GEMS, Vol. Three**
        C. M. Kornbluth and others

G-6   **HORROR GEMS, Vol. Three**
        August Derleth and others

If you've enjoyed this book, you will not want to miss these terrific titles…

ARMCHAIR SCI-FI & HORROR DOUBLE NOVELS, $12.95 each

ARMCHAIR SCIENCE FICTION & FANTASY CLASSICS, $12.95 each

If you've enjoyed this book, you will not want to miss these terrific titles...

ARMCHAIR SCI-FI & HORROR DOUBLE NOVELS, $12.95 each

D-71   **THE DEEP END** by Gregory Luce
         TO WATCH BY NIGHT by Robert Moore Williams

D-72   **SWORDSMAN OF LOST TERRA** by Poul Anderson
         PLANET OF GHOSTS by David V. Reed

D-73   **MOON OF BATTLE** by J. J. Allerton
         THE MUTANT WEAPON by Murray Leinster

D-74   **OLD SPACEMEN NEVER DIE!** John Jakes
         RETURN TO EARTH by Bryan Berry

D-75   **THE THING FROM UNDERNEATH** by Milton Lesser
         OPERATION INTERSTELLAR by George O. Smith

D-76   **THE BURNING WORLD** by Algis Budrys
         FOREVER IS TOO LONG by Chester S. Geier

D-77   **THE COSMIC JUNKMAN** by Rog Phillips
         THE ULTIMATE WEAPON by John W. Campbell

D-78   **THE TIES OF EARTH** by James H. Schmitz
         CUE FOR QUIET by Thomas L. Sherred

D-79   **SECRET OF THE MARTIANS** by Paul W. Fairman
         THE VARIABLE MAN by Philip K. Dick

D-80   **THE GREEN GIRL** by Jack Williamson
         THE ROBOT PERIL by Don Wilcox

ARMCHAIR SCIENCE FICTION CLASSICS, $12.95 each

C-25   **THE STAR KINGS**
         by Edmond Hamilton

C-26   **NOT IN SOLITUDE**
         by Kenneth Gantz

C-32   **PROMETHEUS II**
         by S. J. Byrne

ARMCHAIR SCIENCE FICTION & HORROR GEMS SERIES, $12.95 each

G-7   **SCIENCE FICTION GEMS, Vol. Seven**
        Jack Sharkey and others

G-8   **HORROR GEMS, Vol. Eight**
        Seabury Quinn and others

A YEARNING TO RETURN HOME...TO EARTH

There had never been any space flight. It was against the law! The Astronomical Institute had decided ages ago that it was impractical, and that no attempts should be made to break out of the Venusian gravitational field. And so space flight was made...taboo.

So people the world over accepted this as fact. It was what they had been taught; it was what they believed. Citizens went about their daily lives with the firm belief that the human race had originated on Venus thousands and thousands of years before, never dreaming the truth, never guessing that humanity's roots led back to Earth. But there were a few men who had doubts— just a few. Men like Mike Woolf, Kerry, and Rennig. Men who were—curious.

CAST OF CHARACTERS

MIKE WOOLF
The only thing he had wanted was to get a hold of the forbidden books—and what he found was unbelievable!

RENNIG
He invested many years of his life toward the completion of Gissing's rocket in the hope of someday launching to Earth.

KERRY MAXWELL
Too loud, too thoughtless, too fond of drinking, he really didn't think much of those Earth people—drunk or sober!

DR. ERIC GISSING
He worked for twenty-two years in secrecy—with the threat of imprisonment hanging over him the whole time!

WILLA
She was the old, withered leader of the last vestige of humanity, and she faced a decision no mother should have to make.

THE OTHERS
Disfigured mutants, giants and dwarfs alike, who were at constant war with the last remaining humans on Earth.

RETURN
TO EARTH

By
BRYAN BERRY

ARMCHAIR FICTION
PO Box 4369, Medford, Oregon 97504

CHAPTER ONE
Mother Planet

The First Library was shrouded in mist and twilight, and thin, hot, steaming rain. It stretched several hundred yards along the highway, set back from the road, quiet, lonely. And inside...

Mike Woolf snapped the button on his torch when he heard the footsteps.

He pressed his body back against the wall and waited, counting the footfalls as they passed above him, heavy footfalls, several pairs of them.

It would be the Library guard passing on its routine inspection. He had timed it all perfectly: his entrance, gaining the Rare Books Section, then the shifting of the flagstone and the descent.

Perfect.

The footsteps passed away. There would be no more until morning, unless the vault had burglar alarms, and that was doubtful. The guard itself was merely a matter of custom; even the Library officials did not quite know why it was done. The point was that there had always been a guard over the Library and as far as they were concerned there always would be. It was the custom.

He switched on his torch again and the magnesium beam slitted the darkness with a knife edge of brilliance.

All around him was dust and decay; old metal boxes piled up, metal chests, pieces of curtaining and rugs and spiders' webs; and squeakings from small, scuttling creatures in the corners.

He walked along the corridor between the piles of boxes, treading softly, carefully, keeping his torch low, looking from side to side with eager eyes.

More bales, this time of decayed, worm-eaten wood, a few more tin chests and then a little anteroom leading off from the main vault.

He walked into it through the space where a door might once have hung. A flight of crumbling stairs led deeper. He went down.

The air was thick and stifling and got worse as he neared the bottom of the stairs. There was no opening for air to get in, of course; he could hardly expect anything better.

The stairs came out into a smaller vault and Mike gave a gasp when he saw what it contained.

"The books. Oh, the books!" he breathed.

And there they were. Piles of them stacked on the floor, packed away in transparent airtight packets. He picked one up and blew away the dust. The label on it read: SPACE TRAVEL.

How many centuries had they been there untouched, unseen? He put the torch between his teeth and was about to tear away the seal from the packet when a sound startled him.

Footsteps again—somewhere high above him!

He ran for the stairs and went up them in the darkness three at a time, gained the anteroom and paced quickly across the main vault, mounted the first flight of steps and stood listening. The footsteps had died away.

All was still again. He eased the flagstone gently to one side and peered up.

Darkness.

He climbed out of the vault with his prize under his quivering arm. Carefully he put back the great stone, straining, easing, lowering. Then he started through the Rare Books Section towards the main corridors. The way through the silent building seemed interminable and little trickles of excitement and thrill were crawling on his spine like ants on a dry stick.

A sound. Somewhere a door banged and a man's footsteps sounded distantly. Mike stopped and melted with the shadowy wall. He started to edge along softly, making no sound, his torch switched off.

Darkness and silence.

So dark it was, and so silent. He edged round the corner with the precious books clutched tightly to his body. Just a few more corridors and then the outer door and away.

His tongue between his teeth he eased himself forward, step by step, inch by inch.

One corridor—still no patrolmen. The second corridor.

The third…Light blinked in the distance over the outer door. He stole up to it softly, softly, took his employee's globe from his pocket and fitted it to the depression in the lock. The door swung open.

Behind, the towering mass of the First Library Office loomed dark and bleak. A wind swayed the trees. Thick clouds, as always, covered the sky, blanketing the night. And the hot rain trickled down.

Mike locked the door behind him and heaved a sigh. It was over, all over. He had done it at last. No more planning, no more plotting. He had succeeded. There was little chance of being caught now.

He walked away from the Library in the shadow of the trees, trying to concentrate on keeping out of sight, trying not to jump and shout with the joy of what he had done.

To steal the forbidden books! To have three or four of them under your arm and not be caught! It would probably be years before anyone discovered the theft, if indeed anyone ever did. Nobody knew the old books were there. They had rested in their dust and in their age for centuries. *Centuries.* It had been an unbelievable stroke of luck that had led him to them in the first place, luck and the strange curiosity that so few people shared with him.

Kerry and old Doctor Gissing had shared it, but now Gissing was in prison and there were only the two of them left to read and study and explore and ponder on the history of their race. And Kerry was—well, awkward, somehow. He was too loud, too fond of drinking, too thoughtless. It had been pure chance that had drawn them together, and Mike found himself wishing, more than once, that he was alone in his strange quest. For to Kerry it was no more than a game; indeed all life was just a game to him. And Mike often wondered whether his friend would win or lose that game.

It had always seemed strange to Mike that so few were curious. Most people, young and old alike, seemed content to take things as they found them—or as they were made to find them. Not Mike.

And now he had actually got hold of four *books*. It was wonderful.

He reached the highway and walked down towards the shadowy grove where his beetle was parked, hidden away among the trees and bushes. He pressed the starter button and glided away up towards the city, feeling warm and pleased and eager, eager to tear away the protective coverings on the books and read, read, *read!* It was like being a boy again on a Christmas morning—seeing the stocking overflowing with presents, wanting to open them yet not wanting to spoil the pleasant agony of suspense.

He got in about three and started to read. He was due at work in the First Library Office in the morning at seven but he could not help himself.

He ripped the covers off the books. Now he would *see*. He had always sworn that there *were* such books, somewhere. That was why he had taken the job in the First Library to start with, and that was why he had spent two whole years planning this theft as soon as he heard about the vaults below the building, for if the books existed where would they be but there?

And now he had them in his hands, or some of them, anyway. Perhaps he would be able to get more—but these would do for the start.

The first book was an historical work of some kind. He looked at the title and date and the publisher's imprint and sat back amazed.

Quite crazy. Printed in somewhere called London, England. No such place existed, that was certain.

He ruffled the pages and looked at the text. His frown deepened. Crazier still—places and people and events that had never happened, never been. The book was one big lie. He looked at the index, searching for names he knew.

There were none.

There was nothing there he knew or understood. The whole book might have been the historical record of another age, another world...

He looked at the date. Printed in 1966. Well, that was only about four centuries ago. Let's see now, 1966, that was before the year of the Comet; what were the Venusians doing *then?* His mind went racing back through little alleys of schoolbook learning. That was about the time of Ruler Karl and Ruler Martin. Yes—and the early Night Side explorations for radium and mellium.

Mike frowned and put the book down on the table. He pressed the food conveyor button marked 'Coffee' and the little hatch opened. He took out the plasticup of steaming coffee and the plate of doughnuts and started to chew absently.

This must all be a hoax. Yet if a hoax why all the secrecy? Why did no one officially know about the books and why was there an armed guard over the Library? This guard had been maintained for so many years that nobody knew what they were for anyway.

The problem was crazy.

He opened the second book. The problem got crazier.

It was a great, thick work on astronautics, of all things. Not just a piece of imaginative theory but the real goods. A practical book.

But it couldn't be a practical book. There had never been any space flight. The Astronomical Institute had decided ages ago that it was impractical and that no attempts should be made to break out of the Venusian gravitational field. That was why Eric had been imprisoned—for trying to launch a space plane in secret.

Space flight was forbidden. Mustn't touch.

Again, why?

He returned to the book.

"This," he said aloud, "is a direct contradiction to everything I have been told. Therefore I should throw the book away. It is a useless and possibly dangerous fantasy." He turned over the pages, gazing at the intricate diagrams, trying to follow the complicated mathematical formulae that spattered the pages, looking at the photographs.

The photographs!

Photographs of space ships being launched, photographs of long, thin, cylindrical objects flaming into the sky. And the sky was clear, too. No clouds. Another impossibility. Venus had clouds all the time. The sky was never clear, there was always the cloud and fog. No sky *could* be clear on Venus. It was like saying that water wasn't wet. Crazy.

The third book made him feel worse. It was an atlas.

He finished his coffee and ruffled the pages as he lit a cigarette.

Names he had never seen before, countries and continents he knew did not exist, rivers, seas, lakes, mountains—all unknown. And then he turned to the front of the book and saw a picture that he recognized instantly—a map of the planets and the sun.

Since the Absorption Beam had been invented astronomers had been able to see the other planets of the system through the clouds. The map was plain. Very plain. It showed the exact positions of the planets in relation to the sun at a given time. Below the map, which unfolded out of the book, were the words: MAP OF THE SOLAR SYSTEM, SHOWING THE POSITION OF EARTH, RELATIVE TO THE OTHER PLANETS AND THE SUN.

Earth!

No, no! It couldn't be! He stubbed the cigarette out in the ashtray and swallowed once or twice; or he would have swallowed if there had been any saliva to swallow, but his throat had dried up. He found he was listening for sounds— any sounds. Anything to take his mind away from the map and the words.

Earth. That pinpoint of light that astronomers said was probably a dead world. And here was a book printed on that world. And no one had ever built a space ship to cross the gap. Interplanetary travel was impractical.

According to all the rules he should term the book an idiotic fantasy and destroy it. Why, then, did he feel like reading on and believing?

So this was the secret he had unearthed. Yet what was it? That foolish people had written foolish books that were without meaning—or that they had written the truth and others had seen fit to cover it up?

The fourth book was a diary, a personal diary of someone called Short, Captain John Short.

Mike read quickly, turning the old, old pages hastily, yet careful not to destroy them in his haste. The diary told of a great voyage in a giant ship, sailing with two or three others.

It was a personal account, and dealt mainly with people rather than with any technical details. Apparently the writer was the captain of the vessel.

He read on and on as the clock ticked away the minutes and the hours. He took a second cup of coffee from the conveyor hatch.

Slowly, like water trickling through a crack to fill a cave, the truth came to him.

This was not just an ordinary voyage he was reading about.

It was a voyage in space. *The* voyage.

The voyage that made some sort of sense out of all he had just read. The great trek from Earth to Venus that must have been made by his ancestors!

So that was it.

The Earthmen had come sixty-seven million miles to Venus.

But why did nobody talk about it—why all the secrecy? What was wrong with coming from Earth?

He read on and found out.

It was the *last* voyage he was reading about. The last voyage made from a dying planet. There was a war, waged with weapons he did not quite understand but which must have made the planet a boiling hell. Just a few ships had set off in the midst of all the blood and chaos, filled with refugees from all countries, all creeds. They had sawn space in two and roared into the inky darkness to land on and colonize his own planet—Venus.

Some sort of memory block must have been created in their minds to remove all recollections of Earth and the voyage, to prevent them from thinking of Earth or of ever wanting to return there. An artificially created amnesia.

Thus the whole history of his planet, stored in books, in pictures, in men's minds, was false; no more than a blind pulled over the truth; a false memory installed to fill the vacuum created when memory of Earth was removed.

Mike stepped across to the televisor and dialed a series of numbers. There was a pause, then the screen lit up.

Kerry Maxwell blinked uncertainly at him from the white square on the set. His eyes were red and half-closed. His pajama jacket was flapping open and there was a glass in his hand.

The voice came thickly from the visor.

"Mike! What in heck's the matter? Do you know what time it is?"

"This is important."

"So is my sleep."

Mike frowned as he saw Kerry stumble and drop the glass on to the floor.

"Listen, can you come round tomorrow?"

The face on the screen creased up into a frown, the brows drew up taut together, the eyes, red-rimmed, glared up from under. "I'm not in the habit of accepting invitations at four in the morning."

"Never mind that. Can you come round?"

"What's the matter?"

"I can't tell you over the visor. Just come round tomorrow."

"Well, okay."

The screen went blank and there was silence in the room.

Mike thought of the books again, and in doing so he forgot Kerry with his bleary eyes and his flabby, hanging face, forgot the strange, unpredictable ways in which his mind worked, forgot about the many times he himself had sworn to break with him.

They had waited a long time for this, though. A long time, but it was worth waiting for. Everything tied up. It had to be true. It all explained so many things. The guards at the

Library not knowing why they had to be there, the ban on space travel experiments. Everything.

He wondered if any of the high-ups really knew about it or whether they acted the way they did because *their* fathers had acted thus, and their fathers before *them*.

How far did the history of the planet really go back? Dates were meaningless now, if it was true. Everything was meaningless except Earth.

That was when he really started to think about the old world—*his* old world. The real home of the Venusians.

What would it be like now? How would it have changed? Would there be any life there at all, and if there was life what would it be like?

So many questions and no answers. So many, many, questions.

And he thought about space, too. The coldness of it, and the dark. The flaming jets tearing through the clouds, roaring up beyond the atmosphere, beyond gravity, beyond everything.

He picked up the book on astronautics again. It was called: ASTRONAUTICS FROM A TO Z. With a book like that to guide you, and perhaps others, too...

No.

No, the idea was crazy, *crazy!* It couldn't be done. Now Doc Gissing was in prison it would be impossible unless his old assistant could be tracked down and...

No.

Forget it. Forget it all. Let it just be theory and study, tracing back the history through the books. That would be difficult and dangerous enough. But it *would* be wonderful to...

"This is nutty," he said aloud. "I'm screwy to be thinking things like that. Of course nothing can be done about Earth now. Thousands of years have probably passed since that last voyage. It will be a dead planet now."

And the thought made him sad. Earth dead; revolving and revolving endlessly, aimlessly, up there beyond the clouds. Dead and dry and rusted up. The sort of weapons the book described would surely kill a planet. There could be nothing living up there now—could there?

The bleak walls of his room did not answer.

CHAPTER TWO
Three Men Alone

There is no night and day on Venus. Venus does not turn like Earth; she keeps her face towards the sun always, and her face is hot and steaming and covered with the sores of volcanoes and the wrinkles of chasms and the wet mouths of bubbling lakes. Her back, facing outwards into space, is cold, eternally, icily cold. Between them lies the Twilight Belt and it is there that the cities stand.

The First City sprawls awkwardly with buildings in half-circles emerging from the center, like the legs of a dead spider. And there is the First Building, too. It stands apart from the streets and parks and trees; stands gaunt and dark and there is a high wall about it, and there are guards stationed at all the gates in this wall. For it is here that the Rulers live, the Masters, the Prime Ministers, the Kings.

The three men stood looking out at the sprawling twilight city; stood together beside the crystal window, their beards jutting, their eyes somber through responsibility, through overwork, and perhaps through fear.

For these three men were the only ones who *knew.*

They knew all the secrets of Venus's past as their fathers had known before them, right back to the first ruler of Venus. And nobody else knew. Nobody at all.

The first man turned.

"Sometimes I wonder whether it is the right thing after all," he said.

"Of course it is the right thing. What else could we do?"

"We could lift the ban on space travel experiments."

"And have everyone wonder why it had ever been banned at all?"

"Well, we could do something."

"Not yet. It isn't time, yet. They are not ready for it. In another hundred years..."

The three men stared out of the window at the city, stared and thought of the time, so many years distant, when their descendants might be able to tell the truth at last.

The first man touched a button near the window and a plastiscreen came down over the crystal pane, erasing the night as a rubber erases a pencil mark.

There was so much on the shoulders of these three men, so much knowledge that they could not impart to others, so much shame at not being able to tell. But the people were not yet ready for it. They could not yet be told of Earth and the great wars and the journey through space.

And the knowledge burned in the Rulers' minds with a steady, biting flame that never died.

If you had looked all over Venus you wouldn't have found three lonelier men.

But the Rulers had always been lonely, for theirs was the power and theirs the knowledge. In the old days when the colonists had first landed and the scientists and leaders had banded together to form a temporary government the chief scientist had said: "We must devise a way of forgetting Earth, forgetting everything that has happened. We must think of a plan to rid ourselves of everything concerning Earth. We are Venusians now, not Earthmen, and we must remember that and only that."

And a plan was devised. The amnesia.

It was very simple. In that year 1999 the scientists were very clever men, and one of them put the plan before the Ruler. The Ruler approved it.

'But there is one thing,' the scientist had said. 'Surely you will agree that *one* person ought to know what has happened? This amnesia will take away all recollection of Earth and will substitute a false history that we have been assembling over the past few months. But we feel that somebody ought to be left who would know about Earth and everything.'

The Ruler at that time had been a very courageous man. He had said: 'I agree entirely. *I* will be that man.'

And that is how it happened.

And now these three brothers, descendants of that first courageous man, looked sadly at each other's shadowed eyes, saw the crow's feet etching the pallid skin, saw the nervous twitching and the look of despair lying like ground mist on their faces.

The first man looked across the room at the date, shining from the luminous calendar on the desk. August 5th, 2399. Only four centuries since the Earthmen had landed, since Venusian history had begun. And no one must know, no one must suspect. The lies must be told again and again until the people were wise enough to be told the truth, or could be allowed to travel out into space and perhaps visit their mother planet.

It was a wonderful thought, that. The three men thought of it often. Sometimes they would talk of it, the adventure that they would never see, the voyage out again, back to Earth, back *home.*

On the wall the visor buzzed suddenly. The second man answered it. A man in a tightly fitting uniform appeared on the screen.

"A report has come through from Fourth City, sir. It concerns the man Larmann."

"Well?"

"The police are satisfied that he has been circulating literature on the possibility of travelling through space, sir."

The second man's face clouded. "They are *sure?*"

"Yes, sir. Quite sure. They found a number of pamphlets in his house."

"Very well, Mavor. Send the report through to me and hold the man in solitary confinement." He snapped the button down on the visor and the screen went blank again.

The room was silent. The first man turned to the second and his eyes asked a question his lips would not form.

The second man looked down. "We must. There is no other way. We cannot let him go on spreading this literature. Now we are certain we shall have to act."

"You are sure?"

"You heard what Mavor said."

"There couldn't be a mistake?!"

"I fear not."

"Then...?"

"I'll go through the file just to make certain, but I have little hope. Larmann has been a trouble in Fourth City for some years. First that political business and now this."

"Do you think he *knows* anything?"

"No, probably guesswork and curiosity. But he'll have to go."

"Go?"

"Well, you know what I mean."

They both knew what he meant. Larmann would be executed. There was no other way.

In the far, far distance there sounded the rumble of a volcano, momentarily drowning out the sounds of the city. A reminder that Venus was yet young. And the clouds swirled about the planet and made it sparkle in space like a precious jewel, if indeed there were eyes left on the other plants to watch the heavens and minds left to wonder...

And that was Venus. A new world pretending it was old, with three tired, lonely men leading the people they knew not where. And everybody else going about their work thinking that their race stretched back thousands and thousands of years, not dreaming the truth, not given any cause for doubt or wonder. Except for just the few. Men like Mike Woolf or Larmann or those who had gone before them. Men who were—*curious*.

CHAPTER THREE
O! Dream of Midnight Space

Kerry came round to see Mike the next evening. This time he was sober. He came up in the lift with a shadowy, worried look on his face. What in Hades had Mike wanted, calling at that hour of the night? Not that he remembered it very clearly, but even so...

The building was held in evening quiet. Outside there was the subdued hum of the beetle cars and the occasional roar of planes. Inside there was stillness.

Kerry pushed the buzzer outside Mike's door.

The voice from the robot lock whispered, "Who is it, please?"

"Kerry."

The machine registered his vocal tones, checked them and clicked the admission switch all as Kerry shifted from one foot to the other. The door slid aside. He went in.

Mike was sitting in the window seat with a tray of coffee by him and a small pile of books.

"Hullo, there, glad you came."

97

Kerry threw his mackintosh into the dryer and walked across the room. "Now what is all this? What possessed you to call me up at that crazy hour last night?"

"Give you three guesses."

"It must be important."

"It is. I've proved my theory, Kerry. I've got hold of some of the books."

"The books?"

"Yes."

Kerry looked down at the volumes on the little table, saw the lettering of their titles and felt the silence of the room webbing round him, saw Mike's eager face peering up expectantly. There were the books. Right there on the table. The books.

"So you were right."

"Yes. See? What did I say all along? If there had ever been any of the books they were bound to be in the old vault below the First Library. I got them yesterday night."

"But what *are* they?"

"They're all we ever asked for—and more. They're just incredible, Kerry. You'll have to read them."

"Yes, but what…?"

"Read them and see."

Kerry sat down and turned the books over and looked at the titles again. Then he started to read.

The minutes and the hours tiptoed softly by in the room. Mike drank cup after cup of coffee as he watched Kerry reading. And Kerry read on and on and on. First picking up the history, then the diary, then the atlas, then the book on astronautics.

Kerry didn't speak at all. He kept his head down and read, burning words that leapt and danced on the pages and formed up into strings of fantasies, rows of incredibles, lines of impossibles. At the end of two hours he looked up.

"Is it true?"

"What else can we think?"

"But then all the history we are taught—it's all *false!*"

"Yes."

"But how was it done?"

"Amnesia, I should think. That would account for all the secrecy. They made everyone forget about Earth and substituted a new history in their minds—a history of Venus."

Kerry lit a cigarette. "But what about the books, how is it that they were left for someone to find?"

"Perhaps some of the people escaped the amnesia. That seems the safest bet. Or perhaps just one person, who helped, one day, that someone might find the books and wonder about Earth."

They looked at each other in silence. For Kerry the thing was momentarily too big to think about: it was like a volcano blowing up around you, leaving you standing there not knowing which way to look, which way to turn. It was frightening.

"So we came from Earth?"

"That's the way it looks."

"Then—then we must have come quite recently."

"I suppose so. Supposing the Earthmen landed in 1999…"

"You mean the year of the comet?"

"Exactly. Our history books tell us that in that year a small planetoid was drawn into Venus by gravity and the contact wrecked the chief cities, destroying most of the buildings and ancient monuments. Now if *that* had all been put into the minds of the colonists in place of the memory of Earth—why, they wouldn't think to question, wouldn't wonder why there were no relics from the past, no buildings, no ancient temples. *They* had all been destroyed in the explosions. It's as simple as that."

"And we're the first to know?"

"I wonder."

"What do you mean?"

Mike looked out of the window. "I mean just that. I wonder if we *are* the first. Perhaps others knew before and were found out."

"Well, anyway, what can we do about it all?"

Mike hunched his shoulders and sipped at his coffee. Shall I tell him what I want to do about it? Shall I tell him I want to go back to Earth, and see what the world is like now, after all these centuries?

"I was thinking of looking up old Gissing's assistant."

"What for? Do you think he knows anything?"

"He might. Gissing once hinted that he knew more than he ever talked about. There might be something there."

"Is he still down at the old laboratory?"

"I don't think so. When they put Gissing in prison the lab was shut up and the staff all left. What was that assistant's name?"

"Rennig, wasn't it?"

"That's right, yes. Rennig."

They spent the rest of that week tracking Rennig down. They found him in a big block of service flats on the edge of First City. He was young and pale and red-haired and he seemed auspicious when he opened the door to them.

"Well?"

"Remember us? Friends of Dr. Gissing?"

"Oh, yes."

They went inside and settled on the sofa while Rennig got them drinks. When they were all seated Mike said:

"I know you were working with Dr. Gissing on his space flight theories and I—"

"I'd rather not discuss it." *Snap.* Just like that.

"Oh. Well if you're sure. You see we thought that as you had worked so closely with Gissing you might be able to help us."

He was wavering. Mike pressed home.

"It's like this. We were friendly with Gissing. He used to tell us that if his experiments ever came to anything he would let us know. Then he got himself put in prison and that was that. But Kerry and I both think his experiments *did* get somewhere and he never had a chance to tell us about them."

Rennig gave a nervous smile. "And you want me to tell you about it all?"

"That's the idea."

"Supposing I refuse?"

"Then we go away without showing you some books you'd give your life to see." Mike waited for the words to sink in. They sank.

"Books?"

Mike nodded.

"What do you want to know about the experiments?"

"Whatever there is to know. Did he ever build a space ship—did he ever do all those things he planned?"

Rennig smiled a strange smile. "If you like I'll show you something. It's a long way from here. But it's worth it."

They stood up. All of them. Taut and waiting, knowing that some great thing was going to happen.

"We're ready," said Mike simply.

They went outside and climbed into Rennig's beetle. Soon they were whirring smoothly off along the wet roads, their pink lights cutting through the mist and rain, passing the concrete and plastic offices and flats and hotels and stores. Whirring out into the twilight towards the dark. Towards the Night Side.

"These books," said Rennig, lolling in the driver's seat, "What are they?"

"Oh, just books."

There was silence again and they sped on. Mile upon mile; through First City, Second City, up on the raised highway that led out to where all days and nights were midnights.

Mike clutched the plastic briefcase that carried the books and hunched himself further back into the corner of the beetle. He began to wonder whether he had been wise in telling Rennig about them. But there was nothing to worry about, really.

He hadn't said anything much. Just that they had some rather special books. Nothing much. And anyway—what were they going all this way to see? Had Gissing ever completed a space plane and could it be out here on the Night Side? Or was it all some sort of trap or a joke?

The beetle ran off the main road and began to skim across the cold, flat plain that ran into the Night Side. Rennig leaned back.

"You'll find the heater switch to your right, Mike. I've had special heating fitted to withstand some of the cold out here."

Mike pushed the switch, thinking: So he comes here often? Why? What does he do out here? Where are we going?

In spite of the heating it got colder. Twilight faded and they crept across into eternal night. Clouds filled the sky and Mike wondered again about Earth. Fancy being actually able to see the stars and the planets. You would be able to do that on Earth. See them all with your naked eyes, without any Absorption Beam or high-powered equipment. To see the stars...

"We're here," said Rennig. He pulled the beetle to a halt and they looked out of the windows.

It was a long building, sprawling and dark, with a bit of a tower sticking into the mist at the back. On a second look the tower wasn't such a 'bit' after all.

It might be big enough to hold a space ship.

"You'll find some quilted suits in the back there. I should wear them. It's mighty cold out here."

They opened the slide below the seats and drew out the suits. In front Rennig was climbing into his.

Like awkward bears, lumbering, they emerged from the beetle and walked with Rennig towards the building.

Inside it was dark. Rennig switched on fluorescent tubes along the wall and they saw the laboratory. Rows of metal switches grinning from the benches like silver teeth, glass tubes, everything.

And there was a small door.

"Does that door lead through to—to—"

"So you saw?"

"I guessed."

"Yes. That leads to the main laboratory and the tower." The three men walked across and into the main laboratory and stood looking up at the silver hull of the ship, resting like a shining fish, standing on its tail.

"I've been working on it since Gissing was taken off. It's almost finished."

"And he never told us."

"He didn't dare tell anyone until it was finished. None of his other assistants knew about this place—only me. I used to come here most evenings with him, after his ordinary work was done."

Here it was then. The last great experiment. The rocket ship.

"It works?" Mike almost whispered the question.

"I don't know. It should. About a month's more work on it and it will be ready for space."

"You're going to try?"

A veil dropped over Rennig's eyes. He spoke softly, quietly, carefully. "I might," he said.

"Let's go somewhere warm where we can talk," said Mike. Rennig took them back into a small room adjoining the laboratory. There Rennig turned on the heating and the globes in the four corners of the room glowed hotly. The men loosened their suits and lit cigarettes.

"Now let's see these books," said Rennig.

"First tell us something about the place here. Did Gissing build it, or what?"

"It was originally one of the old beldenium mines, probably over a hundred years old. Gissing needed somewhere for his experiments apart from the laboratory in First City. He came down here and fitted this place up on his own. When they imprisoned him I had to carry on."

"Had to?"

"*Wanted* to. Now let's see the books."

They showed him the books. Like them he wouldn't believe at first. He argued and blustered and called them idiots and said that such things could not be. But he was wrong. They argued back and explained and pointed out and, after a long time of talking and smoking cigarettes and feeling the room grow warm around them, convinced him.

"That's why we looked you up," said Kerry. "We wondered just how far the experiments had got."

"You mean Earth?"

"That's right."

Rennig was silent. Suddenly everything became possible. He had felt the fear and sadness growing on him as he completed the rocket. At first there had been the flame of enthusiasm and eagerness, but as the work neared completion he had felt very alone and frightened. Where was there to go, now that he had his ship almost ready? Which planet, which world? And now these men had come out of the night and told him fantasies that were not fantasies, told him things that were great and wonderful.

He had a place to go to.

"All right."

"You mean you *will?*"

"Yes."

"When?"

"As soon as the ship is ready. I need another month or so, then I can tell you for certain. You say you got these books from the First Library?"

Mike nodded. "Yes, from the vault underneath it."

"Can you try and get more?"

"Yes. I'll try again tomorrow or the night after. I want to get as many as I can. Not just the textbooks and things but other books as well. I want to find out what Earth was really like."

Rennig smiled. "It's probably different now."

"Probably, yes. But we don't know. There might be life left. We can't be sure."

They got back to First City at three in the morning.

The next night Mike went again to the vault in the quiet and the dark. He took three packages of musty books and brought them to his flat without anyone seeing or suspecting. His luck was too good to be true.

There were books about poetry, natural history, philosophy—seemingly *everything.* He looked at the pictures in the natural history books and marveled at the strange creatures, the dogs, the cows, the elephants, the giraffes, the gorillas that looked so like men. To think there might be some still living on Earth, and he might see them!

He went with Kerry and Rennig to the laboratory on the following night and took the books with him.

"It's wonderful," said Rennig.

"Sure it is," replied Kerry. "But let's go and see this rocket ship of yours. I want to see how it works."

So they left the books and went through into the tower where the rocket stood patiently waiting its day of conquest, of supremity.

"She works on liquid oxygen and new mellium oxide mainly. The subsidiary tubes run on liquid oxygen and MV fuel."

"Maximum velocity—is that what MV means?"

"Yes."

"I've heard of it, of course, but where did you get it? I thought it was unreliable?"

"They've stopped making it now. Dr. Gissing got some about five years ago, raided a fuel store factory over in Fifth City. It's too dangerous for general use. We can't run the main tubes on it for fear of an explosion."

"Can we go inside?"

"Of course."

They climbed the metal ladder and Rennig unlocked the door. Inside there was the smell of electricity and metal and machines. They had to climb another ladder to the control room, because the bottom of the ship contained the fuel tanks and the tubes themselves. Inside the control room Mike looked round.

"I'm not well up in these things. You'll have to explain it all to me before we start."

"There's not much I can explain," said Rennig. "Everything's so damn complicated. Besides which most of the controls are automatic. Outside vision is by television— the cabin is on gimbals—air valve over there—additional oxygen valve over here. On the panel to your right you can see the gauges for gravity, acceleration, fuel consumption, air pressure, temperature."

Kerry walked to a screen on the wall. "What's all this?" he said, banging the screen with his hand.

"That's the course screen. When we're in space it will tell us our position and automatically warn us of approaching asteroids and meteorites." Rennig lit a cigarette and glanced at Mike. "Do you know how long Gissing worked on this?"

"It must have been years."

"Twenty-two years. And no one knew a thing about it. Not even you two!"

"It's a wonder the police never found out when they arrested him."

"That's where he was clever. He kept all his theoretical work in his study at the First City laboratory. That's what the police found. After he admitted experimenting in *theory* and revealed his notes they didn't ask any more questions. They locked him up."

Mike and Kerry moved about the control cabin, touching this, examining that. Fingers trembling with wonder and sometimes with fear at what it was all about and where they were going. They moved like men in a slow-motion dream and Rennig leaned against the door and watched them, smoking silently, dreaming himself of that day not now so far distant when there would no longer be the walls of the laboratory tower about the ship, when there would be walls only of black midnight space.

Each evening they spent in the laboratory and the ship. When they were not working on the ship itself they were sitting in the heated study, reading the books of another world, reading about strange places, strange creatures and about ideas and theories and thoughts that were old when the Venusian First City was yet unborn.

"Listen to this, Kerry," said Mike one night. "It's from a book written when the Earthmen first reached out into space."

"When was that?"

"In 1973, after their third war, when they sent the first ship to their moon. Listen—" and he read:

" 'It is the coming back again that is so wonderful. The return through the greatest night imaginable, through the night of space. Man can talk of the adventure and the power and the majesty of flying out to land upon another world like the Moon but there is nothing so grand as the homecoming, nothing so strong and so strange as the pull of Earth, not to the ship through gravity so much as to the mind through emotion.' "

Kerry put down the book on Earth history and laughed nastily. "You know—you're getting almost an Earthman yourself, what with all this reading and brooding."

Mike did not laugh.

Kerry went on, his great face breaking open in a gash of smile, his voice deep, hearty, strong, a *Venusian* voice: "Now the way I see it is this—it's like one of those early expeditions into the Night Side they made back in 1960—just an adventure."

Mike said quietly: "There wasn't any 1960 for Venus."

"Hades!"

"See what I mean?"

"Yes. Yes. I guess I do. Still, that doesn't alter my point. Here we have a brand new adventure staring us in the face, something nobody else has ever done, a wonderful opportunity."

"Wait. Somebody *did* do it once."

"Eh?"

"The Earthmen."

"Well, you know what I *mean*. Nobody on Venus has done it before at any rate. And here you sit as sad as sad. Why, supposing we do get to Earth. We'll have the planet to ourselves. Imagine that! A planet to play with! Let's have a drink on it! Hey, Rennig, let's have a drink!"

In bed that night, between the warm, gently rippling covers which should have sent him instantly to sleep, Mike lay thinking. Now there was time to think. Before, in the laboratory, talking, reading, attending to this part of the ship, adjusting that part, then there had been no time. But *now*... Was it really as Kerry kept saying? Was he wrong in thinking of Earth this way? Should he, like Kerry, go through space as an adventurer from a distant planet, seeking glory and perhaps riches and power. Or should he go the way he knew he would go—as a man goes when he is returning home— quietly, humbly. And again and again his mind returned to Kerry—big, blustering Kerry with his shouting and drinking. How would things go when they were alone with Rennig in space? How would it be when he couldn't just turn away and forget him, when he was always there?

The rippling of the covers smoothed his mind out, caressed and lulled him to sleep.

From afar came the petulant mutter of a volcano on the Day Side. To Mike, dreaming, it was the blasting of a thousand rocket ships, splashing the night with star-shells, angry red, as the ships all set off home again, to Earth.

So the weeks limped tiredly by and formed together to make a month. In the tower the ship glistened, still patient, still waiting. And Rennig and Mike stood watching her.

"Are you sure everything's all right?" This from Mike.

Rennig nodded slowly. "I've checked and re-checked for two nights, as you well know. There's nothing left now to check!"

"Where's Kerry tonight?"

"He told me he wanted to buy some things to take, said he had to go over to Second City for them."

Mike looked puzzled. "What things? I thought you had all the stores and equipment we needed."

Rennig grunted. "So I have. Perhaps they're presents for the Earthians!" He laughed. "Remember that book you brought with the others—that one about Earth explorers going into a primitive continent and exchanging glass beads for gold or something. Remember? Maybe Kerry thinks he's going to do the same with the Earthians!"

About half an hour later they heard the voice box announce:

"Kerry, let me in."

They let him in.

He had a big aluminum case that they heaved inside, and then they shut the door.

"What's this?"

Kerry grinned. "Presents for you all. The most necessary things in the world for explorers. They're beauties, too."

Down on his knees he went, avidly, like a child wanting to show a new toy to his doting aunt. He opened the magno-locks and threw the lid back.

"See?" he grinned.

Guns.

CHAPTER FOUR
Almost The End

Again the darkness and the silence.

Again the muffled footsteps descending the stairs into the vault, but this was the last time. The *last* time. Just one more night and one more day and then—off!

He was not quite so quiet; not quite so careful as before.

Familiarity with the vault and the stairs made him contemptuous of the thought of capture. Besides, he had heard the guards go round. They wouldn't be round again. They'd all be asleep by now.

His torch flashed across the dark room and he stole among the packages of books. This time he would have to be more discriminating. He would only take books that were of real worth and importance. It would be silly to take just the books he most wanted to read—the novels, the poems, the great books of Earth. No, this time he must take the most useful ones.

He picked up a book that had fallen behind a crate.

With his torch he read the title; SELECTED WRITINGS OF ROBERT A. MENKHUSS. He skimmed the pages— poems, humor—oh, well, he might as well take something for himself. He put it in his pocket. Now where were some on gravitational fields? That was what Rennig needed, wasn't it? Yes.

Ah, *here*.

He picked up the package. Suddenly he felt cold with apprehension. No, it *hadn't* been a sound, had it? That wasn't a noise above him, was it?

Silence.

He started back, quickly, nervously. Up the stairs to the anteroom, through the main vault and up the flight of stairs to the flagstone. He moved it aside cautiously and clambered up into the corridor.

His breath came in sharp little jerks as he stood waiting by the hole. Then he eased the stone back and started through the Rare Books Section with the package of books under his arm.

It was really silly to rush away like this. There hadn't been any sound. No sound at all. He had had time to get more books, he *ought* to have stayed and looked round some more. It had hardly been worth while risking everything just for a package on gravity and one slim book that had caught his fancy.

He rounded the corridor and stopped.

"Hey," said the guard in front.

Mike turned and a numbness came down on him out of the air. 'Caught, caught, caught!' pounded his heart. He started to run.

The guards came after him, running, too. They had their guns in their hands and they were catching up on him.

"Hey, there, stop!" one shouted. "Who are you?"

Mike saw the incinerator waste hatch in the recess by one of the crystal windows. Gasping he ran up to it and thrust the package of books inside. There—now they wouldn't know about the books at least. He started to run off down the corridor again but the delay had cost him his short start.

They caught him as he tried to open one of the side doors with his employees' globe.

"Now, what is all this, eh?" Two of them held his arms while the captain in charge asked the question.

"All what?"

"Don't start that. I want to know what you're doing here. Don't you know no one's allowed in here after six? It's against the rules."

The fool, the fool! What does he know about it all? He doesn't even know why he's here guarding this place. He doesn't know about the vault or anything. Just a dumb captain. And he has to catch me!

"I'll have to take you in," said the captain. He slipped a pair of metal cuffs over Mike's wrists.

"Hey, now, what's this?" He reached forward and took the slim book from Mike's pocket. "Stealing books, huh? Now you're in *real* trouble. Know the penalty for stealing books? Prison."

Prison. Ha! Does he know the penalty for stealing books like *that?*

"Come on, boys, bring him along."

They took him to the guard office on the second floor and sat him down and gave him a cup of coffee.

The captain went over to the visor and dialed a number. The screen showed an office and a fat police officer with glasses.

"Captain Reynald, sir, Library guard. We just picked a man up here."

"What?"

"Yes, sir, picked a man up. First time it's happened, isn't it?"

The fat man's eyes bulged. He was in no mood for humor.

"Keep him there under guard, captain, under *heavy* guard, understand? On no account leave him, whether he's in irons or not. I'm sending a beetle over for him right away."

Mike saw the fat man's hand reach for his desk phone before the screen went blank.

The captain sauntered back from the screen and sat down opposite Mike. "Now, tell me, what were you after? Just this one book? And what did you put down that chute?"

Not a word. Don't tell him anything. Keep your mouth shut. Wait until there's a chance to make a break for it.

"Well, if you won't talk you won't." The captain yawned and picked up the book, ruffled the pages and then looked at the title page. "What is this—a joke?" he asked. One of the other men walked over.

"I should think it must be, sir."

"You know what?"

"What?" said the guard.

"We haven't searched him yet."

They set to work, took his papers and his money and his keys and then his employee's globe.

"So you work here?" He looked through the papers.

"Michael Thomas Woolf, aged twenty-seven, clerk at First Library." The captain put the things carefully on the table and sat down. He yawned.

Minutes later the police headquarters' beetle drew up outside and they heard doors slamming and muffled voices.

The fat inspector bustled in, panting. Behind him a dozen plain-clothes men, at his side a small, tired-looking man with a tired-seeming voice. Mike recognized him from photographs in the papers and from the telescreens. Harvey Doles, head of the Venusian police.

"Now who is this man, captain?"

"Good evening, sir, he's an employee here. Name's Michael Woolf. We found him in the south corridor with some books or something under his arm. He pushed them through an incinerator hatch before we could stop him. He had one in his pocket, though."

The inspector picked the book up and glanced at it. Then he conferred with Doles in muffled whispers.

"Bring him outside. We're taking him back to headquarters. Leeson, Wright, stay here and look after the guard. Captain Reynald—we shall need you."

They bustled Mike out through the door and down the stairs and out to the waiting beetle. The door closed. The beetle started up and the mist closed in on them.

Mike sat, manacled, in the back, his eyes closed. So this was it. All the planning, all the dreaming, all the adventure gone like smoke in the summer air.

At headquarters he was pushed roughly into a chair while the fat man fired questions.

"What were you doing there? Don't you know it's against the rules to be in the Library after hours? Being an employee is no excuse. *All* employees check out at six and are not allowed back until the following morning. You knew that, didn't you? *Didn't you?*"

Of course I knew it. Of course. But you don't even know why the rule was imposed at all. None of you do.

"Will you answer me?"

Mike sat and stared in front of him. The fat man blustered on.

"You realize, I suppose, that you have committed a very serious offence, and one that isn't likely to be punished lightly."

Then Doles came in from the little room at one side. He stood looking at Mike with a tired smile. He addressed the fat man thus:

"Do you know what you're supposed to do in circumstances like this?" he asked.

The fat man stammered and went a little red. "Why—er," he started.

"You're supposed to put a call through to First House."

"First House?"

Doles walked across to the visor and pushed a blue stud at one side. The screen flashed PERSONAL lettering across and then showed the reception office at First House.

"Police Headquarters, First City. Doles speaking. Man picked up in First Library. According to Emergency Precaution Rule 33 this should be reported to First House and relayed instantly to the Rulers."

The startled clerk nodded. His face worked for a second and then he blurted: "Yes, Mr. Doles. Right away."

Doles waited and watched. The clerk plugged into the interbuilding sub-visor. They saw the relay screen light up.

Doles spoke sharply to the clerk. "Put me through quickly, man."

The screen blacked out and lit up again showing the First Ruler. "Well, Doles?"

"We've picked a man up in the First Library, sir. According to the Emergency Precautions we have to report to you personally."

A little cloud seemed to drift across the dark face, the eye grew dim and tired and the voice, when it answered, seemed tired also. "Bring him straight over."

The screen went blank. Doles turned away and looked at the fat inspector with distaste. "Now get that beetle ready again."

Lights blazed in the First House. Mike slumped in the back of the beetle once again. Tired, he was, and numb, now. At first he had watched every move his captors made, waiting for a chance to escape, to run anywhere, away out into the night. He felt the power of the police machine wearing on him. And now—the First House and the Rulers. Did they know, then? Or was this just a matter of form, a custom handed down from the old days?

Doles sat beside him, smoking a cigar. The man's watery, tired eyes never left him. There would be no escape now. No escape. No more journeys to the Night Side. No more looking up at that slim silver pencil that was to have carried him and his dreams across sixty-seven million miles of space and utter darkness. No more watching the clouds swirling here on Venus even, or walking its streets or drinking coffee and smoking in his own flat. No more anything.

They took him in the lift to the office floor and then, alone with Doles, he waited in one of the small reception rooms.

A voice box said, "Enter, Woolf. Mr. Doles, please stay where you are. We shall call you if we need you."

Mike stood up and walked towards the gilt door, which slid aside as he approached. He went inside.

They were there. The three of them. Their beards jutting, their faces the same as in the telescreens and the papers.

But they weren't smiling now, they weren't waving to the people or reading speeches or attending receptions. They were silent and solemn and grouped together like three dark statues, brooding.

"Woolf?"

"Yes."

"Sit down."

He sat down.

The Second Ruler was shorter than the others. He moved more quickly, his eyes were more alert. He walked across to the chair opposite Mike and sat down, looking at him closely. One of the policemen had given him the book Mike had stolen. He held it in his hand.

"You know what this is?"

It was useless to lie to him.

"Yes, I know."

"Where did you get it?"

"In the vault below the First Library."

The three Rulers exchanged glances. "So *that's* where they were. I thought they must still be somewhere. If we'd had any sense we'd have looked there."

They all looked at Mike again. The First Ruler spoke.

"You *know?*"

"I know."

"I want to explain, Woolf. You have seen the books, presumably. You know about Earth and everything."

"Yes."

"Well, then, I'll try and explain why you've been brought here. What you have found out is secret. That's the first thing. It's secret because it must be so. It has been secret ever since memory of Earth and all that happened there was taken from Venus. It must stay secret."

Mike shifted in his chair. Where now were all the thoughts of Earth and the arguments for going there? He felt numbed with the fear of what was to come, felt somehow that nothing mattered now. The tiredness became a great giant thing that crushed out the words that formed in his mind before they could get to his lips. He sat and listened as the Second Ruler's words flowed about him.

"Four centuries have passed since the Earthmen landed. The Rulers have had to keep the secret for that time. Venus is not ready yet to know its own history. It is still too young, too immature. Indeed it is likely that it will never know."

The First Ruler went to the visor and spoke to a secretary in one of the other rooms.

"Carden, I have a job for you. Below the First Library there is an old vault. You will take a squad of men and destroy everything you find there. You will personally see that nobody has time to examine what they destroy and you will also see that nothing is taken out of the vault by any of the men. Search them as they leave. Then fill the vault with autofreeze and seal it.

The screen went blank and the First Ruler turned to Mike.

"Mr. Woolf—we have tried to explain why you have been brought here. Now it is our duty to tell you what is to happen to you." Their eyes turned from him, they fingered their beards, they looked not so much like Rulers as men who have to punish their children for something they might have done themselves when young.

Mike knew what was coming. He knew he would not be allowed to live, *could* not be allowed to live. He was a menace to the quiet and calm of Venus now. The knowledge that was his would not be allowed to spread further.

"You are sentenced to death."

The words seemed unreal. Everything seemed unreal—the last journey to the Library, the guards, the capture, the police. Everything.

He found himself nodding, as though he understood it all, as if it was just the luck of the game.

He was taken outside while the Rulers spoke for a while to Doles. Then Doles came out and they walked through the building to the lift. They went down and Mike was taken out to the waiting beetle.

Off again into the rain and mist, through the deserted streets to Police Headquarters.

Had he been wide awake Mike might have noticed the roads and the buildings he was passing. But he was not wide-awake. The fear of death had come down on him, and the tiredness had increased. He didn't realize that Kerry, having waited for him for so long at his flat, had at last come out of the apartment block and was cruising back in his beetle to his own flat.

The beetles passed each other on Highway Nine, midway between the First House and the Police Headquarters. Mike, in the back of the police beetle had no reason to glance out and watch the passing beetles for possible rescue. He didn't see Kerry.

They pulled in at Police Headquarters and Mike was taken inside and locked in a small cell. He knew there would be no execution until the morning or possibly the afternoon. That was all the time he had left—a few hours. And he didn't want to die. He didn't want to see the green room with the vents along the walls through which the gas would come. He remembered reading an article about the green room in one of the papers—all about how you go in and stand wondering where the gas would come from and then you see the vents and then you know you haven't any more than twenty or thirty seconds left in the world. Seconds to count and one special second shortly coming to dread. Just time to think of the many, many bad things you have done and time to wish you hadn't done them.

The cell had a little cot and a table, polished so that it shone. One wall was gray and sparkling. Mike knew it was a sheet of one-way glass. On the other side the guards would be sitting, watching him pace the floor, watching him lie on the cot, watching him perhaps cry.

He straightened up.

This was no way to go on. How about those books he had read? Books about Earth. The novels and the poetry of Earth. Did men break down and cry and become afraid of death? They did not. They were brave, the men of Earth. Had they not set out into space and beaten space and landed here on Venus? Were *those* fellows afraid of death or of anything? No, of course not.

It was just that he was dying for a cause. He felt he was like that man in the book who had died so that others should live.

On the other side of the one-way glass wall one of the guards saw him with his chin in the air and his eyes blazing. The guard laughed a great sarcastic, throaty laugh that came, muffled, to Mike in the cell.

The laugh seemed still in the air as Mike fell on to the cot and covered his face with his hands.

Outside, in voices that they thought he could not hear, the guards talked.

"What exactly *is* the guy in for?"

"I don't know. It's an Emergency Precaution Sentence. Straight from the First Ruler."

"From the First Ruler?"

"Yes."

"Well! Fancy—from the *First Ruler!*"

"Must be some sort of political offence or something, I guess. But whatever it was it must have been bad. The green room at three tomorrow afternoon."

"Boy! Am I glad I'm on *this* side of that glass."

"Me, too."

"Hey—didn't you have a bottle of something in your pocket?"

"Yes."

"Well, let's get at it before the relief guard come in."

Sounds of a cork coming out of a bottle, and liquid, gurgling noises as two glasses are filled up.

"Shall I take one in to him?"

"Naw. Old Harry's on relief guard. If there's any over, leave it for him."

"Okay. Well, down she goes."

Contented drinking sounds, then. Gulping sounds. Happy sounds. Then another silence while the guards stretched and finished their beer. Then feet tramping—the relief guard. Uniform capes thrown to the ground with wet, swishy sounds. The stamp of heavy boots. The brief, grunted greetings.

"Thought you were going on morning guard."

"No. Changed last minute. Richards is sick."

"Oh. *Say,* know who we've got in here?"

"No?"

"Fellow in on Emergency Precaution Sentence. Yes, straight from the First Ruler."

"No!"

"Yes."

"Well, *imagine* that!"

Mike felt them all looking through at him. Looking just the way he might have looked at a pet that had savaged its master and was going to be destroyed. Just that very same way.

CHAPTER FIVE
Escape and Away

Pat, pat, pat went the footsteps along the corridor. Kerry trod lightly but by the time he reached the door of Rennig's apartment he was panting. He paused to get his breath and then pushed the buzzer.

"Who is it, please?"

"Kerry."

The robot lock connected to the alarm vibrator and Rennig, stretched on his bed, felt and heard the sound. He sat up.

"Well?"

"Kerry."

With a bound he was up and across the room and at the door.

Kerry was wet with the night rain. He stood dripping and worried on the doormat.

"What's the matter? I told you not to come tonight."

"They've got Mike."

Rennig's eyes were gummy; he had the hot, sticky taste of sleep in his mouth. "Who are *they?*"

"The police."

"The *police?*"

"Yes."

"Where? How? What for? How do you know?"

"Well, I waited down at his place for ages. He said he'd be there tonight and we were going to talk over one or two things. Anyway, he didn't turn up, so after waiting awhile I started back to my flat in my beetle. I was up on Highway Nine, just turning by the Museum buildings, when a police beetle passed me—and Mike was inside."

"You're sure?"

"Of course I'm sure. He was sitting slumped in the back."

Rennig's mouth tightened into a white scar. He walked to the window and stood looking out at the mist. "On Highway Nine. What do you think they could have picked him up for?"

Kerry shrugged. "He said he was going down to get some more books tonight. Just as a last effort. If the guards picked him up there…"

"If they *did,* he'll be on an Emergency Precaution charge. And you know what that means."

"The green room?"

"Yes. The green room. Oh, why did he have to go down for the books again? Why did he have to risk everything?" Rennig saw the dream of Earth cracking up all about him. All the plans, all the hopes, all the adventure—gone in the air like dust. "Now, let's see—if they picked him up in the Library they would take him to Police Headquarters—but then what would he be doing on Highway Nine?"

"Well, whatever he was doing there he'll be back at the police building by now," said Kerry.

"Yes."

"And they won't give him much time before…"

"You're right, they won't. We've got to get him out."

So they stood there and thought about how to get Mike out of prison.

They thought long and deeply and at last Rennig said: "You know what happens when they get an Emergency Precaution charge?"

Kerry said: "No?"

"They execute within twenty-four hours. Always. It's the rule."

"Then what are we going to do?"

Rennig turned away from the window and started to walk about the room, his brow pleated up in thought. "We're going to get him out, and quickly, too."

Kerry's face started to quiver. An ice of perspiration formed on his brow. He was thinking about the guards and the prison walls and the thought of having to break in and rescue Mike...and the risk of death loomed up, a black shadow in his mind.

His fingers shook as he lit a cigarette and puffed smoke out into the room. "How *can* we get him out? We've got to have a plan. Can you think of a way? The prison is sure to be guarded. With an important prisoner on an Emergency Precaution charge the place will be seething with guards."

Rennig moved across the room and started to unlock a small cabinet that stood against the wall. "I have something here that will deal with the guards. I'm not a scientist for nothing."

He fumbled open the door of the cabinet and squatted on his heels in front of it. Kerry watched, trembling, his eyes brilliant in that bright room.

Rennig took out a long tube with an attachment on the end—something that looked like a transmitter valve.

"What is it?"

"Just a gun."

"What does it fire?"

Rennig smiled a sly smile. "Oh—just fuel."

"Fuel?"

"M.V. fuel."

"Eh?"

"They decided M.V. fuel was unsuitable for a very special reason, Kerry. It reacts with oxygen almost instantaneously. It forms a peculiar substance that hasn't got a name yet—a sort of mist that solidifies within fractions of a second."

Kerry frowned. "But how can you use it as a weapon?"

"This frozen mist is colder than ice—and harder, too. It freezes solid anyone you fire at."

"That's all very well, but we've got to get *into* the place before we start shooting the guards."

Rennig dialed a number on the visor. Central Information Office showed on the screen. "Can we help you?"

The girl looked so natural—it was hard to think she was all gleaming metal and oiled bearings below the evening gown. It was hard to think of the face as being rubber and plastic and putty.

"Show us a map of Area Nine, First City."

The screen blazed brilliantly and showed a model map. Rennig switched off the transmission before he spoke. Then:

"There's the Police Headquarters buildings." He pointed.

"Yes."

"We go straight there and go all out to rescue Mike. If one of us gets caught the other tries to get to the laboratory and off."

Kerry shifted from one foot to the other awkwardly, uneasily. There was tension in the room, excitement, fear and urgency, spinning taut webs between the two men.

"So if we have to split we try and make Earth alone?"

"That's right. *Someone* must get away."

"So how do we go about it all?"

"Well, see the map? See the two overhead roads leading up along the railway? There's a slope that leads down to the outer wall of the police building. We go round the side, pierce the wall..."

"Pierce it? How? What with?"

"Needler cutter beams."

"Where do we get *them?*"

"I've got three here. I used them on the Amery expedition to the Night Side and never took them back to the laboratory."

Kerry rubbed the wet palms of his hands together. "Yes, then what?"

Rennig turned off the visor before replying.

"Well, all the police buildings are built on the same plan. There are the corridors and offices round the outside and the prison is in the center. If we pierce the back corridor walls we can get straight through into the prison with the needlers. Then use the freeze stuff on any guards and get Mike away as quick as we can."

"And straight to the Night Side?"

"Of course."

"Aren't you forgetting something"

"What?"

"All the police beetles are faster than civilian ones. If we don't get a good start on them we shall be caught before we're out of the Twilight Zone."

"Then we take a flier."

"Where do we get a flier at this time of night?"

They stopped talking and thought about it. There was no time for them to get to the airport, and even if there had been it was doubtful if they could have got one to land on the Police Headquarters' roof.

"Know anyone with a private flier?"

"Well, yes," said Kerry. "But he's not likely to lend it at this time of night."

"I wasn't thinking of *asking* him to lend it."

"You mean just take it?"

"If we're going to Earth nobody will be able to have us up for it, and if we get caught at this rescue game we shall have other things to worry about."

"Okay, then. The man I know lives on the corner of Twelve and Fifteen. The flier's parked on the roofdrome. Question One—how do we get up to the roofdrome? Question two—which one of us is going to drive the damn thing?"

"I can drive a flier and we get to it by lift and by giving your friend's voice into the robot lock. Can you imitate him?"

"Hell, no! Anyway that doesn't work. I've tried it before."

"What does he sound like? High voice? Low voice? What?"

"Low, deep down, rich sort of voice."

"Like this— 'Kerry here, open the door?' "

"Hey—that's not bad. But he's deeper than that—more cultured."

"This then— 'This is Kerry here, open the door?' "

"Almost. It might pass."

Rennig tried again.

"So-so."

After three more goes he was almost perfect.

"Where did you learn to do that?"

"I used to be an actor, did two years of repertory in Third City, then I gave it up to be a scientist. Look where it's landed me! Now, listen, say we get the flier first and get down to the police building. Then what?"

"We cut through the outer wall. Right?"

"Right. After that...?"

"After that we take Mike to the flier and get him away to the laboratory as fast as possible."

"Then what?"

"Presumably we start for Earth."

Rennig walked across to a built-in cupboard, pressed a switch and waited while the door slid aside.

"I haven't much of that M.V. fuel here. But there's enough for the gun." He took a small cylinder out of the cupboard and connected it to the gun with a length of rubber tube. "There's enough M.V. here to deal with the entire police force of First City, though. It's sealed off in compartments inside the cylinder, and compressed as well. When one compartment empties the next is automatically opened."

"What about the needlers?" said Kerry.

"They're here." He drew out three stubby weapons.

"So we're ready?"

"Yes."

Rennig changed from his sleeping suit into an all-weather outfit and then they both took up their weapons and their rain capes and Rennig opened the door.

"It seems funny that I shan't be corning back here, ever. It's too crazy to be true."

"But it is true. If we succeed in rescuing Mike and getting him to the ship you won't see Venus again," Kerry said it bitterly: already fearful for his own life; already regretting the whole thing.

"And if we fail to get Mike I shan't see Venus again, either."

They stood by the open door and the weight of the adventure pressed down on them from the ceiling and the walls of the silent room. They felt suddenly the meaning of it all—saw the shape of Earth looming ahead like a great dream yet to be dreamed. And they saw something else, also.

A small, green room.

The night was dark and cold and wet and misty, as it always was. There was nothing different about this night. Men and women slept their usual sleep; small winds whistled their usual whistles round the buildings; rains fell gently the way they usually fell.

Kerry and Rennig drove the beetle down towards Highway Twelve in silence. The motor purred to itself and not to them, the road swished under them, swishing to itself alone. The mist hugged itself, not them.

They had their own thoughts and they thought them in silence in the beetle, not noticing the motor's hum, nor the wet road swishing, nor the mist seeking to clutch and to claw them.

They thought the thoughts all men think when they are risking their lives. Thoughts like: 'Is it all worth while? Am I going to get anything out of it? If I am not going to profit, why am I doing it at all?'

Thoughts like that.

They arrived at Highway Twelve and pulled the beetle into the drive by a hotel.

"He lives here. Third floor, I think. His room number is three-0-seven. Hey—supposing there's a porter on duty and—"

"We tell him we're calling to see your friend. What's his name now?"

"Lawrence. Bruce Lawrence."

"Well, there we are."

"But supposing he calls Bruce's room and announces us?

Rennig smiled. "Then we go up announced and use the freeze on him."

"Not on my friends, you don't." Kerry's face crinkled up into a frown. "Nobody freezes my friends."

"Would you prefer him to call the police?"

"Well..."

"There you are, then."

They went up the steps to the hotel and walked through the arch. A porter was sitting behind the reception desk.

"Yes, sir?"

They noticed the metallic *clacking* of his voice. A robot.

"We'd like to see Mr. Bruce Lawrence. It's urgent. Can you call him, please?"

The robot plugged in the visor to Lawrence's room and the watchers saw the screen blur for a minute before

Lawrence appeared, hair over his eyes, robe thrown over his shoulders.

"Who in hell…?"

"Two gentlemen to see you, sir."

"Who are they. Who goes visiting at this time of night?"

Kerry stepped forward. "It's Kerry, Bruce. And it is important."

"Oh, it's you. Well, come on up."

The screen went blank. They started for the lift.

Inside, Rennig said: "Would you rather sock him than freeze him?"

Kerry nodded.

"Okay, then, that's what we do."

They got out at the third floor. The door opened before they got there. Bruce stood with his robe fastened round him, gazing at them with a small, puzzled frown.

Kerry hit him with the butt end of his needler and he went down on the rubber floor with a sound like somebody dropping a bag of walnuts. He stayed down.

"Now, push him into his room, shut the door and let's take the lift up to the roof."

So they did that.

On the roof it was misty and Kerry had difficulty in finding the main door of the hangar.

"Here we are. Now do your impersonation act. And it had better be good."

Rennig stepped up to the door. "Bruce Lawrence here. Open up, please."

There was a pause.

Rennig stood away from the steel door and sighed. Four hundred years before, on Earth, he might have prayed.

The door slid aside.

"We've done it. We've done it!"

"Keep your voice down. We've got to get the thing out first."

They got the flier out. They wheeled it to the edge of the hotel and then climbed inside.

Kerry pushed the starter and the motor swirred, muffled under the metal bonnet. Then they were away. Above the hotel, above the street, above First City. Above and away.

"Where are we going to stow the flier?"

"Right down there, on the raised road by the police building. When we've parked it we go down that slope and start on the outer walls."

They brought the flier down gently and carefully and hid it in the shadow of a great empty building.

"Down this slope, now. Careful."

They left the flier and walked down the slope towards the police building. Lights were glimmering in the windows— stray lights, dotted here and there over the dark bulk. Lights that meant policemen and danger and perhaps death.

The wall loomed ahead out of the mist. A black wall; a solid wall—a *very* solid wall.

"Try your needler on it here. It's as good a place as any. I don't see how we can judge where the main corridors inside are. We'll just have to trust to luck."

Kerry got the needler from his pocket and glanced about him. "Do they have guards outside these places?"

"I don't know—don't waste time."

The needler made a glowing point on the wall, like the end of a cigarette, now like the end of a cigar, growing, growing. Kerry turned the gun in an arc and the metal and stone walls glowed hotly and began to crumble.

"Supposing a guard comes along now? What do we do then?"

"Use the needler on him. Now hurry with that wall."

Kerry hurried with the wall and the gap was soon wide enough. They stole inside.

"If this is the outer corridor the prison cells will be roughly straight ahead. You'd better start on that wall now."

Kerry switched the needler on again and the wall crackled away like tissue paper.

And not a guard did they see. There was the silence of the grave clinging to the rooms through which they passed.

"Now, somewhere here there should be a guardroom and then the cells. Don't use the needler any more—we'll try these doors."

They tried the doors.

"Psst."

"What?"

"Voices. Behind this door. Keep your voice down."

They pressed close to the door and heard the muffled tones of men talking coming to them like the distant murmur of breakers.

"This is the guardroom, then," whispered Rennig. "Now, listen—when I give the word take a shot at the lock with the needler and I'll push through with the M.V. gun. You back me up and needle anyone who tries to get away or raise the alarm."

Kerry nodded, his lips trembling, his face white with fear.

He directed the needler at the lock. It glowed red. They heard the voices stop and there was just the faint, faint, whine from the needler reaching peak power. There came a *click* from the lock. Rennig pushed the door open and stepped inside.

"Hey—what the...?"

Rennig steadied the M.V. gun and fired. The compressed fuel spread in a fan-shaped spray across the room and one of the guards froze with his gun in his hand.

One wall of the guardroom was one-way glass. Rennig saw Mike slumped on the bed at the same instant that the fat guard, who had been asleep on a cot at the far end of the room, woke up.

"Hey, there… Who *are* you?"

Kerry turned the needler across. The man fell with a small, smoking hole in his middle. The other guards stayed where they were.

Rennig said: "I'll keep the rest of them covered, Kerry; you get Mike out."

Kerry turned the needler on the edge of the sliding door of the cell and walked inside. Mike jerked in his sleep.

"Get up, Mike!"

"Wha—what?"

"It's me, Kerry!" Urgently shaking him.

"Kerry?"

Mike lurched up to his feet and stood blinking and rubbing his eyes. Kerry urged him out.

"How about the other guards?" asked Kerry. "If we make a dash for it they'll sound the alarm."

"Don't worry about them. Look" Rennig gestured with the M.V. gun.

The guards were standing *very* still.

"You mean…?"

"Yes."

Kerry looked at Rennig for a long, silent second and Mike said:

"You did this?"

Rennig nodded. "It was the only thing to do."

"Well, now we've got to be getting out."

They went the same way as they had come.

The flier took the three of them high into the mist above the slumbering buildings of First City. Up, up, they went, and then turned in the eternal twilight and made for the Night Side.

Below there was no sign of awakening or alarm, no sign that the City knew what was happening. And in the Police Headquarters frozen men stood and stared at nothing with eyes that could not see.

It took them most of half an hour to reach the laboratory. They grounded the flier, then, and ran across the frozen ground to the entrance. The tower pointed up into the sky, pointing the way, the way upwards and skywards and Earthwards. Mike shivered when he saw it and realized how near he had been to never seeing it at all, how near they all had been.

The door slid aside at Rennig's command and they went inside.

"Now get the space suits out of the storage and bring them through to the tower. I've got a hundred things to do before we can start. And we *must* hurry. As soon as they find Mike is missing they'll organize a search. We've got to be away within twenty minutes, and that's cutting it too fine for comfort."

Rennig disappeared towards the tower and Mike and Kerry started to drag the heavy space suits out of the storage cupboard.

"Makes you feel like a kid again, doesn't it? All this preparing," said Kerry.

"Yes, it does."

"I've got that same feeling in my stomach I used to have on that first day at a new school, when you don't quite know what everything's all about, when it all seems a big dream."

Mike shifted a space suit on to his shoulder and started for the tower. "But this is one dream you don't wake from."

They were all ready. Rennig stood by the ladder. The ship gleamed and sparkled and shone. The ship stood there, knowing it was her field day and reveling in it all; stood proudly saying to the walls of the tower: 'Look at me; take a *good, long* look. You won't see me tomorrow, you walls who have watched and waited for so long. You won't see me again.

Rennig said: "Now we're ready. Hey, wait—what are those boxes there?"

"Books," said Mike.

"What books? I've got all the books we need now; packed them away the other day. What are *they?*"

"Some Earth books I want to take with me."

"Don't be a child, Mike. We're over maximum load already. If we take any more we risk failure and a good many other things besides."

Mike frowned. "Then why take those guns?"

"We may need them."

"What for?"

"Well, we don't know if there's anything living on Earth."

"Men, you mean?"

"I didn't say so."

Mike took two of the boxes from the pile. "I'll take these and leave the rest."

Rennig shrugged and then started to climb the ladder. Kerry followed him, then Mike.

"What about the roof of the tower?"

Rennig grunted. "I've seen to that. It's plastic. We shall go through like a pencil through paper. No, there's nothing else now."

Mike stood in the doorway for a moment and looked down at the great silent laboratory. And he could almost see a gray misty figure standing below him like a shroud of vapor, the figure of an old man—Dr. Gissing.

And Mike said, softly, to himself, and perhaps to the ghost, too: "Here we go, old man. Here we go." Then Rennig called out and Mike stepped back and climbed into the control cabin while the door was sealed.

"All the instruments are set," said Rennig. "Belt yourselves in."

They strapped themselves to the gravity cots and waited. Rennig stood at the panel and muttered: "Ship sealed. Air Pressure Normal, Engines, Automatic... Power, Automatic... Course... Automatic again. Right." His hand fell suddenly on the main power switch. There was a great lurch and the Course Screen lit up, showing a tiny dot of light moving, slowly, slowly.

Kerry closed his eyes. He needed a drink—oh so badly he needed a drink.

They didn't notice the roof burst as they passed into the mist and the night.

With a roar of the great rockets they were away in a rush of air and a lick of red fire, rising up hugely above the laboratory, away, away...

And below a gray, wispy ghost-wraith figure that no one could have seen waved a sad goodbye.

CHAPTER SIX
Voyage in Eternal Dark

Whoooooooooooosh! Lying on the gravity cots the men felt the pull, stretching their mouths like elastic bands, pressing their heads down on the pillows, making their minds buzz like hives of humming bees.

Mike lay and strained against the vicious pull as the acceleration increased. He turned his head this way and that way but nothing stopped the humming and the buzzing and the merciless pressure.

136

He seemed to feel some great hand squeezing, *squeezing,* pressing the control cabin in about his head, pressing his head in about his brain and his nerves and his eyes.

Then the colors of the ship started to run and the shapes of things became blurry and unsure, wavered and faded and receded and came back starkly.

Then everything became dark as he closed his eyes and gave up fighting back.

There came a humming, an intolerable humming. Then, quietly, surely, the pressure ironed him out and left him stretched out on the cot.

And the pressure did that to each of the men. Ironed them out. Left them.

And the ship soared up through the mist leaving its red trail in the sky as a scarlet, pointing finger moving in darkness. A ship blind now to the pull of Venus, blind to the rushing clouds, blind to all except the surging upwards and outwards into the greatest darkness of all.

Minutes later they passed out of the atmosphere. A bell rang in the ship but no one heard. They didn't have to hear, anyway. The ship was on Automatic Drive. The clucking robot control plotted the course set out beforehand.

The ship was silent and smooth. It glided through the dark like a bird soaring, effortlessly.

Mike stretched out one hand, then the other. He groped for a minute and then sat up. Shapes in the room shuddered, expanded and contracted, grew dim, grew bright, grew dull, grew brilliant.

He shook his head and gazed at the vision screen.

Stars.

Stars shining steadily, without the twinkling seen through the Absorption Beam telescopes.

So they had done it. They had broken through at last, broken away from Venus—out, out towards Earth.

Rennig groaned on his cot. "What happened? I can't see..."

Mike heaved himself up and went over to where Rennig was lying, half in the cot, half sprawled across the small desk.

"Here—wake up, Rennig! We did it, we *made* it. We're out in *space!*"

Rennig stood up. "Mike—check the air pressure and supply, then get Kerry out of that cot." He pointed. "His nose has been bleeding. Mop the blood up."

Rennig turned and started to check the course on the small screen.

"You can see the stars out there."

Rennig stared at him. "Of course you can."

"They don't twinkle. They burn steadily."

"That's because of the lack of air. It's only the atmosphere that makes them twinkle when you see them in the A.B. telescopes."

"Doesn't it *do* something to you—seeing them like that, and seeing space, too?"

Rennig seemed surprised. "What, for instance?"

"Oh, nothing." Mike walked across to the air gauge.

When they got right away from Venus peculiar things started to happen. The food capsules floated off the table, Rennig's pen soared up to the roof of the cabin.

Kerry poured a jug of water out and the water formed a globe in the air.

"Hey—look at that. Just like a kid's balloon. Watch *this!*"

He hit the globe with the flat of his hand. It broke up into a myriad tiny globes which flew hither and thither. Where the tiny globes hit something a fine mist of still smaller globes was formed.

"See—? Just like back home! Mist everywhere."

"We may need that water, Kerry. If something goes wrong we may need it badly."

"Sure, Rennig. But it is *funny*, isn't it?"

"Is it? It's only the lack of gravity. Is *that* funny?"

Once the initial checking of instruments had been done there was little work to do on the ship. She ran on automatic control all the way. Mike read of Earth from the books he had brought. Read or sat staring at the vision screen.

Earth somewhere out there, he thought.

Earth—an old football thrown away into the sky, now just hanging there like a dead thing. How quiet it was and how strange to look out like this at the myriad stars, each one a sun. He remembered the great roar and buzz and swish of the leaving; the terrible *pressing* on him, and then the pain, and after that nothing.

And now here were the stars.

He looked at the screen more closely. One of those spots, those little points of steady brilliance, was Earth.

How long had they been in the ship? He didn't know. Time out here was nothing. It was a thing that you merely talked about sometimes, not a thing that *happened*, as on Venus. No time seemed to pass at all out here.

So this was what it was like, then. Space. The blackness and the emptiness and the loneliness. Even when Kerry was beside him, talking about what they would do when they got to Earth, even then he felt somehow *alone*. It was funny, but there it was.

He began to wonder whether either of the others felt it.

Rennig—over there by the controls, looking at dials that worked automatically; checking gauges that had already been checked, always working, never sitting and reading or taking things easy.

Kerry walked over and slapped him heavily on the back. "Hey—what's up with the dreamer? I'm hungry and we're out of food tablets. Can you go down?"

Mike said: "Okay, then. I'll go."

He went down into the store and ferreted about for the box of tablets, found them and came up to the cabin again. He saw Kerry looking at one of the books—one of the Earth books.

"Were you reading this?"

Mike stood with the case of tablets in his hand. "Yes."

"Well, I don't know. Fancy reading stuff like this!"

"What's the matter with it?"

"It's *silly.*"

"That's great poetry. All of it. It's by Thomas Moore."

Kerry opened the book at random. His mouth twitched. He said: "It's just plain stupid. Listen:

Oft in the stilly night
Ere slumber's chain has bound me,
Fond Memory brings the light
Of other days around me:
The smiles, the tears
Of boyhood's years…

…and so on. It's silly!"

He tossed the book on to the little stool, stood up and walked away.

Let me finish it for you, Mike thought. Let me finish the poem for you. Don't you see? It's just the way *I* feel—that yearning for the past. But the past *I* mean is the past long dead. The past on Earth. But you wouldn't understand that, would you?

He watched Kerry go towards the hatch and descend into the lower part of the ship where Rennig had gone to work on one of the brake rocket tubes that he had thought to be faulty.

Alone again. With nothing about the little ship for a million miles except space.

And Mike read the end few lines of the poem in a low voice; read to the walls and the buzzing and clicking instruments, and to the dark space outside.

...I feel like one
Who treads alone
Some banquet—hall deserted,
Whose lights are fled
Whose garlands dead,
And all but he departed!
Thus in the stilly night
Ere slumber's chain has bound me,
Sad Memory brings the light
Of other days around me.

Rennig was stretched out on his cot with a book on astronautics open on his chest. He turned his head and said:

"We'll be nearing Earth within half an hour."

Kerry glanced up. "How do you mean *'nearing?'* "

"Well, we shall be near enough to see it large against the stars. After that we shall be able to watch it grow larger and larger until it fills the screen. Then we cut out the automatic guide and rely on our brains."

"Huh?"

"Yes."

"But why?"

"It's all very well to set the ship on automatic when you're leaving a planet you've lived on and studied. It's different when you're nearing one you know very little about. We shall only have to run the brake tubes manually. According to my calculations we should be landing somewhere on the continent the Earth books call Europe. We can judge our distance by bounced radar beams and the instruments will record everything else." Rennig turned back to his book.

Mike and Kerry sat restlessly, now knowing that the voyage was ending, now fearing what might yet happen.

And Mike thought more and more about Kerry; about the way he had stowed whisky away in the store and had thrown out boxes of the food capsules to make room; about all the little things he had done and said purely to annoy; about the way he boasted and shouted and sneered. And he thought: 'All these things will one day lead to something bigger.' In his mind he could see the thin shred of remaining friendship breaking and something else taking its place—something *very* different.

The two men watched their leader lying easily on the couch and they said not a word. They sat there and thought all the things men think when they start to realize that a million things can go wrong, anyone of which can mean death.

The time came when the great glowing planet filled the vision screen, when the darkness gave way to the misty light of day—then all was ready.

Rennig dashed from gauge to dial, from machine to screen, from control to notebook. Checking, re-checking; cutting out this rocket tube, cutting in that one.

They felt, but did not hear, the roaring as they neared Earth.

They felt the sudden dreadful jerk as the brake tubes belched into action; felt the bellowing, clacking, screaming hulk of the ship lower herself to Earth like an old man stepping out of a beetle car.

Mike clutched the edge of the desk, then steadied himself, gripping one of the handrails.

And through his mind there raced visions from the books he had read—visions of Columbus stepping onto the continent of America, of all the great explorers, Scott, da Gama—all of them. Earthmen. And suddenly he knew, too, how they felt when, after their years of roving, they came back *home*.

The ship steadied, lurched a little and rested. The tubes were dead. Rennig switched this switch and that switch—off.

Silence in the cabin, save for the little sounds of three men breathing heavily.

"Well, here we are, boys." Rennig smiled at them.

"Yes," said Mike.

"We did it," said Kerry. "Yes, we did it all right. I knew we would. Well, don't let's just *stand* here. Let's get out and see what it all looks like. This Earth we've been hearing so much about—eh, Mike?" He straightened up his rumpled suit.

"Shall we go straight out now?" asked Mike softly.

Kerry sneered. "Sure, why not? Let's go out and show these Earthians of yours what a *real* conqueror looks like. Come on boys, let's open up the door. Come on, come on."

Mike did not look at him as he started to turn the great dial that operated the pressure-locked door below.

CHAPTER SEVEN
The Third Planet

A lot had happened to Earth in the years after the Second World War.

First there had been the mock peace; then, after a decade, the first of the Atomic wars, and the Second Atomic war. Then there was a break. Men gathered their strength for the next war that was sure to come. But the war did not come.

There came instead yet another mock peace, more dreadful than the first. Governments bowed and scraped to each other and set industry to work yet again, forging greater and more terrible weapons to destroy what was left of the major cities.

And nobody believed in anything at all.

And the next war was the last.

But there were some men, still clinging to that strong, strange thing called truth that makes men men, who set off skywards towards a far planet. Just a colony of men and women and children who still *believed*. They flew away and were lost to Earth.

The war went on. But this time men knew that there was no hope of anyone winning. There was nothing left to win, anyway.

And the war stopped not by armistice or total victory but by the spread of plague and disease and famine.

The plague.

Spreading outwards came the plague, crawling like an ugly spider over the land and leaving its sticky trail of sudden and hideous death behind. Crawling through cities and leaving them empty and hollow.

And Man panicked and began to leave the cities and trek over the wastes to other places where the plague was unknown.

And those who left Earth?

They flew away in great space ships towards the evening star that was called Venus. They had hopes, those few men and women, hopes of finding life and peace and freedom. And their hopes became facts and they lived on Venus and, through the amnesia, forgot Earth and the wars and plagues.

But on Earth all those hopes were dying.

And with the dying of hope there also died that veneer of civilization which rests like a cellophane wrapper on the beast that is man.

The plague and the atomic radiations ran through mankind like a butcher with an axe. But the animals seemed unaffected. *Too* unaffected. They multiplied and re-multiplied, the rats and the dogs and the cats and the horses. The rats especially.

And the *shape* of the land was a little different, too. Where before there had been green fields and forestland there was now brown, parched, crackling earth. And there were great craters where the atomic bombs had fallen and in one place—where the flat lands of Holland had rested so peacefully–there was the Abyss.

The Abyss had been formed when the largest atomic pile in the world had exploded at the end of the last great war. It was still active, still a grinning red eye in the night, filled with reacting solids and incandescent gases. Still a warning, still a terror. Men never approach the spot now.

So the whole planet had been thrown away and allowed to get dirty and diseased. And because there was no need for them to remember the people forgot the little band that had set off into the dark night of space. And there was nothing to remind those left behind of the hope and adventure of it all.

But the Earth itself remembered. That small patch of soil, now a gray, sandy, radioactive desert where once the city had stood, where once the great ships had pointed their noses at the sky, and where the emigrants had gathered.

And the Earth remembered the day of their parting, the *great* day.

"They're sealing up the doors now."

"Yes, I know."

"Doesn't it make you rather wish you were going too?"

"Not me, friend. I'd rather stick here on Mother Earth. I don't want to go off to Venus or Mars or Saturn. This place is the place for me, war or no war."

"Do you think they'll get there?"

"Well, they *might*—and then again they might not. But I wouldn't go if they paid me. Those things may be all right for getting to the moon, but the planets are a good many million miles further on. No, sir, not for *me!*"

"Still—it makes you kind of jealous, somehow."

"Hey—there's the raid whistle going."

"Wait for them to blast off. I want to see them blast off."

"Come on, come on. The raids won't wait."

"There they go. See them? There they go!"

Red streaks of flame and the great ships moving upwards, upwards, upwards. And the raid whistles sounded all over the city, welcoming the people to the underground shelters.

But that was a long time ago.

No one remembers it at all. And the papers and books and films that recorded it are dust now, or if not dust they are buried under the rubble of the empty, broken cities.

And the Earthmen themselves? They are very different from those early Lords of Creation. *Very* different. For atomic radiations can do much to change man's appearance.

They live now in tribes and have the little lives, the little loves and wars of the savage and the barbarian. And they stay away from the cities for fear of the plague. They live in the valleys and in the mountains and in caves and in tiny villages and some, the last few remaining true *men,* have been forced to live underground, away from the stronger mutants.

And this was the world Mike and Kerry and Rennig came to, from out of the dark of space.

CHAPTER EIGHT
Prowler in the Night

The door opened and they came down the ladder slowly, the three of them. They stood in a group, hushed together, blinking in the sunlight and shielding their eyes.

"So this is Earth," said Mike.

"This is it," said Rennig, and he started to walk up the slight hill. The others followed and soon they were looking over a small valley where a stream ran through bushes and low, scrubby trees.

"We'd better put glare glasses on; this light will burn our eyes out if we're not careful."

They all put their glasses on and stared about them. The land was dry and the soil loose beneath their feet.

Kerry said, "Oughtn't we to have a little ceremony or something? You know—the first men to reach Earth; raise the flag and go down on one knee. That's what the explorers used to do, isn't it, Mike?"

Mike did not answer.

Rennig looked over the valley. "Well," he said. "There are plants still growing and I saw some small animals over behind those trees. Earth isn't as dead as we thought."

"As *who* thought?"

"All right, Mike. Now we'd better get back to the ship and collect some stores. I don't know about you others but I'd like to spend the night outside for once. The ship gets on your nerves after a bit."

"You're right there."

"Come on, then."

They turned and made their way back to the ship.

"Still think there are any Earthmen left, Mike?"

"How should I know? It's possible, isn't it?"

"Oh, sure—it's *possible.*"

They went back up the ladder.

"Now, what are we going to need?"

"In the store you'll find some aluminum fiber tents, we shall need them, and some food capsules—we shall have to live on them until we find what growing things are good to eat. The vegetation is fairly similar to Venus in appearance but we must be careful. There are two cases of instruments we'd better take as well, I want to make some experiments in the morning."

Kerry and Mike went down into the store and began to sort out the things.

Kerry opened up the case of guns. "We'd better take some of these."

Mike frowned. "What for?"

"Well, there may be wild animals or—or anything."

"Or *men?*"

"Yes, or men."

They took the stores up to the cabin. Rennig was standing by the vision screen. "Come over here and look at this," he said.

"What is it?"

"See?"

"Yes, but what...?"

"It's the fall of night, the sun setting."

"So that's what it's like."

"This planet rotates, unlike Venus, giving you a real night and a real day. See the way the sky is darkening?"

Mike stood and watched the screen like a small boy watching a Punch-and-Judy show. So this was what the poets meant by the falling dusk and the gathering shadows.

"What's that over there?"

"Where?"

"That red glow."

"That's the sun setting."

"No, not there—*there.*" Mike pointed.

"I don't know."

They watched the red glow burn steadily in the sky, over a distant hill. It was not the glowing of the sun, but a more sullen glow, angry and hot and vivid in the evening sky.

"We'd better make camp while there's still some light left."

They took the stores out of the ship and camped on the little hill nearby. They set up the three tents swiftly, laying the electric sleep cushions inside. Then Kerry made coffee and they sat outside the tents sipping it and watching night crawl in over the sky.

"It's peaceful here," said Rennig, sighing.

"Well, it's *home,* isn't it?" said Mike.

"Oh, are you off on that again?" grinned Kerry.

Silence.

Rennig pulled a packet of cigarettes from his pocket and handed them round. "Has anyone thought that this place *really* will be our home from now on?

"Yes," said Mike. "And I don't think it's so bad, either."

They smoked and drank their coffee as the stars started pricking the sky. They saw the moon, too, hanging over the distant hills, gazing wistfully down as she had done since man first raised his hairy face towards the sky. The eternal, proud, watchful moon.

"Do you think there *are* any men left, Rennig?" asked Kerry.

"It's difficult to say. Frankly I doubt it. The wars those books described were bad enough. If they had any after the men left for Venus they would probably be worse. What with atomic radiations and everything I should think the human race is dead here, or at any rate dying."

"What are we going to do tomorrow? We ought to make some sort of plan, oughtn't we?"

"Well, the first thing to do is to find out exactly where we are. We can do that from the maps in that atlas. Then we can do a bit of exploring. I want to find out what that red glow is."

Mike stirred the sandy soil with his foot. "We've got all the time in the world, haven't we?"

"Yes, that's true. All the time in *this* world."

Kerry said: "You know, we're doing this all wrong. Sitting here drinking coffee and smoking cigarettes. We should really be celebrating. Didn't we bring some drink with us?"

Rennig looked up quickly. "You ought to know."

"Well, I'll go and get it and we can have a party. Let's not invite anyone else—just the three of us, huh?"

Nobody laughed.

"Wait here. I'll go get the drink." And Kerry was up on his feet and away across the slope towards the ship.

In a little while he returned bearing a crate.

"Here we are. Plenty of it, too. Get the glasses out, Mike, and we'll all have a drink. Get the glasses out."

Nobody moved.

"What's up *now*? We're going to celebrate, remember?" Kerry squatted and took the cork from the first bottle and poured a little wine into a mug. "Any more of these mugs about? Oh, yes, there they are." He filled the three mugs, then, and handed one to Mike and one to Rennig. "Here's to us!"

"Here's to us."

"Well, don't look so damned *happy* about it all."

"I just feel a bit tired," said Mike as he finished the wine. "I think I'll go in and get some sleep." He stood up and stretched and looked out at the stars glittering in the night sky like diamonds scattered on black velvet. Then he went into the tent.

Kerry poured some more wine out. "He's a funny chap, that Mike, always so moody."

"Yes. Well, I think I'll turn in, too."

"So soon? There's plenty of drink left. We should be celebrating, you know."

"No more for me."

"Hell, yes—let me fill the glass up. *There,* that's better. Now we should read out some dramatic little piece about how thankful we are to have reached here, shouldn't we? That's what they did in those books."

He reached out and took hold of the little book that Mike had brought to read. "Let's see if there's anything suitable here." He thumbed the pages over. "You know—Mike reads this stuff all the time. Poetry! Ha! Here's something." He held the book open and brought his belt lamp up so that he could read.

"Listen to this, will you? It's from a book written in 1973. He read it to me once before, I remember. Listen. "It is the coming back again that is so wonderful. The return through the greatest night imaginable, through the night of space. Man can talk of the... Why, hullo, Mike, thought you'd gone to bed."

"Give me that book."

"What's up? I was only reading a bit to Rennig here. There's nothing wrong in that, is there?"

Rennig looked up quickly. "Now, you two. We're going to see a lot of each other from now on. Don't start quarrelling yet."

"Let's have the book, Kerry." He held out his hand.

"Sure, Mike, sure. There you are."

Mike turned and went back into the tent.

"See what I mean?" said Kerry. *"Touchy."*

And a wind blew across the camp: an Earth wind; coming up from the endless south and blowing over the land towards the northern wastes, where the snow bites the ground forever.

Mike lay snugly in the tent. It was all wrong, so *wrong*, he thought. It shouldn't be like this at all, the return to Earth. It should be somehow more solemn, more respectful. This was home. He heard Kerry's voice raised outside as he blustered to Rennig. He has changed, thought Mike. Changed a good deal. He's different, now; different and he doesn't fit here. He shouldn't have come. Mike thought of the time ahead. Time stretching out into a life of hearing Rennig's soulless voice and Kerry's blustering.

And he turned his head and tried to sleep.

And sleep came.

How long he had been sleeping he didn't know; but something had wakened him. He lay listening.

Silence.

It must be late. The camp is quiet. The others would be asleep. Perhaps one of them had turned in his sleep or something. He listened again.

Yes—there it was. A dull padding sound and a scrabbling.

He eased himself up from the covers and reached for a torch. It was probably Kerry or Rennig out for a spot of air. Maybe they couldn't sleep.

He switched the torch on and stepped out of the tent.

"Is that you, Kerry?" he whispered.

There came no answer from the darkness.

He moved the beam of his torch about the camp. Everything was as he had last seen it, everything in place. Mike walked softly over to the other tents. Perhaps it was some animal browsing round. Perhaps he should go back to the tent and get a gun. Perhaps...

The strong arms came out at him from the darkness and took his throat and mouth. He flailed his hands and tried to bite into the iron fingers that gripped him. Flailed once, and then the hand about his throat released and struck him on the back of the neck.

The darkness became studded with brilliant bursts of light, then, and the world bunched up into an iron fist and fell on him.

He went out.

Dawn clambered up whitely in the morning sky, lighting palely the land beneath. Kerry rolled over and sat up. 'Uh-huh, better rouse Mike, I suppose.' His hand bumped an empty bottle.

He got up and drew his rain cape round him and stepped out of the tent into the watery sunlight. 'Aaaah,' he stretched.

Rennig came out of his tent, washed, shaved and dressed. "Pity we weren't up to see the dawn, isn't it?"

"Yes. Is Mike up yet?"

"I'll go and see." Kerry walked over to the tent and looked inside. "Hum…seems he's beaten both of us and gone for a walk. He's not here."

"Not there?"

"No. And his clothes are there, too. That means he must have gone walking in pajamas. Is that likely?"

Rennig pointed. "What's that?"

Kerry walked over and looked. "It's Mike's torch. And this ground's all roughed up. It looks as though something's happened here."

They stood looking down.

Rennig fingered his lower lip, pulling it out and letting it go. "Something *has* happened. Mike must have come out in the night for some reason and something grabbed him."

"Something?"

"Something intelligent, too, I should say. It would have to have arms to carry him off—and it would have to have kept very quiet to avoid waking us."

"You mean a man?"

"Perhaps Mike was right after all, perhaps there is intelligent life left on Earth."

"You *mean* that?"

Rennig did not answer. Instead be turned and gazed about him, then, after a little sharp silence he said: "Maybe there's something about now—watching us."

Kerry washed and shaved while Rennig took their equipment back to the ship, in preparation for seeking Mike. He left the tents standing, left a supply of food tablets and two M.V. fuel guns and a couple of needlers.

Kerry finished washing and dressing and strapped one of the needlers to his thigh. "Which way do we go?" He felt like saying: 'Do we have to go? Mike's so crazy about Earth—why can't we leave him, forget him. Why should we risk our necks for him?'

"Do you know anything about tracks?"

"No."

"Come here."

Kerry walked across. "Yes, that looks like *something.*"

"It's worth a trial, I should say. See—the earth is disturbed all around there—and that looks like a footprint, and so does *that!*"

They followed the marks past the remaining tent and up the slope. There the ground got harder and the marks were no longer visible. The two men paused.

"What do we do now?"

Rennig pointed across to a cliff face some distance away.

"What does that look like to you?"

Kerry stared. "It looks like *smoke.*"

"And it is smoke. Let's make for the cliff."

So they set off again, winding their way between the scrubby bushes and little gnarled trees towards the white chalk cliff. As they came nearer they saw that the smoke came from the dark patch of a cave about halfway up.

"How do we get up there?"

"Climb."

They started to clamber over the small rocks at the foot of the cliff. Above them the stream of smoke sailed high and thin and strange in the still air. They watched it as they climbed, thinking each his own thoughts as to what they might find when they reached the cave.

The climb was not easy. Twice Rennig slipped back and almost fell; and each time Kerry's great arm steadied him.

They paused on a narrow ledge.

"You know—I should think we've chosen the worst way up this damned cliff. You can't tell me whoever lives up in that cave has to go through this every time he wants to get home."

Rennig grunted. "Well, did *you* see any other way up?"

"No, but that doesn't mean there isn't one."

"Hey, look out there, that isn't safe."

Kerry stepped forward hastily as a little shower of small rocks went puttering down the cliff to land with a clatter on the hard stones beneath.

"Well, if anyone's up there they've heard us now," said Rennig.

"And they may not feel too friendly."

"I wonder if Mike's all right."

Rennig started up the cliff again, catching hold of outcropping rock here and there, hoisting himself up, leaning his weight against the cliff face, breathing heavily, nervously.

Minutes later they reached the cave itself.

"Here we are," said Kerry, puffing as he hauled himself over the edge into the shadow beside Rennig. "Where's the owner?"

"Don't raise your voice like that. If there is an owner we want to meet him in our own time and not before. Now, let's see where this cave leads."

Kerry stood up and caught Rennig's arm. "Wait—look out there."

Rennig turned and looked out at the hills and sky and clouds and... "What *is* it?"

"It's that thing we saw glowing last night."

It was a good many miles away but they could see it all right. It glowed even in the daylight, like an open furnace. And it was big, too; so very, very, *big*.

"What do you think it is?" asked Kerry.

"I don't know. It doesn't look natural to me. I can't tell from here but I should say it's the result of an atomic explosion."

"But those books say the atomic wars ended centuries ago. How can this thing have lasted?"

Rennig plucked his lip. "We don't know what happened after the ships set off for Venus. They may have had many another war here. And if the explosion was great enough..."

"But *what* an explosion it must have been!"

"And what a *war*, too."

They stood looking out at the distant, glowing pit for a second or so. Then Rennig said: "Come on. Let's see where this leads."

And in they went together, into the darkling, shadowed cave.

CHAPTER NINE
The Last Earthmen

When Mike woke he found he was hanging over something with his head brushing the rough grass. He was moving along, too. Whatever was carrying him was walking with strong, smooth, easy paces, covering the ground in long strides, unmindful of the weight of its burden.

Mike thought: "If I turn now, if I twist and throw myself to one side and set this creature off its balance what will I gain? I might manage to run a little way, that is all. Obviously I shall be caught. I have no gun, no weapon; I don't know where I am, nor the direction of the ship. It would really be futile.

And having thought those things he turned and twisted and hurled himself sideways.

Bang went his head on the ground and he heard, dimly, vaguely, the grunt of annoyance made by his captor; saw the great form black against the starry sky. And Mike gasped.

A *man!*

Then a thick arm came down and grasped his leg, even as he tried to raise himself. And the other hand closed into a fist and struck him on the side of the head. Again the little, sparkling, skipping, twinkling lights twittered round his head. Again he lost consciousness.

There was no movement the next time he awoke. He awoke more slowly, too, shaking off, with mental effort, the little pains and little stars that still danced about his skull.

He stretched out his arm and felt the ground. He was lying on some sort of smooth stone. He stretched his legs and turned his head from side to side, remembering the events that had led up to this, remembering and starting to fear...

He opened his eyes, then.

Above him a tall old man was standing, a *very* old man, brittle and yellow with age. Mike looked past him and upwards at the great steel girders stretching this way and that way, all red and rusted and ancient beyond belief. Then he looked at the old man again.

"Sleep now," said the old man.

And Mike could understand the words!

"Sleep." He knelt and stared at Mike and placed a yellow chicken's claw hand on his forehead. "You are tired."

"No, let me up." Mike shook his head and started to his feet. The old man stood back and Mike saw suddenly that there were other men behind, tall men, strong men. He stood there undecided.

"How did I get here? Where am I? What is this place?"

He looked up and about him. The girders stretched as far as he could see, supporting great slabs of concrete. Here and there were piles of rock and concrete and steel, all mixed up like a bowl of stew. And suddenly Mike knew where he was.

'The shelters,' he breathed. The shelters—that must be it. The great underground places the books described—the places where the men and women and children huddled so many, many years before, when the rockets screamed overhead and loosed their rays, their atom bombs, their gas, their death.

It was a vast hall that loomed high above and went away into the dark on either side. And there were lights, but lights so different to the great fluorescent tubes that had once ranged the walls. Now there were bundles of rushes tied awkwardly here and there, casting their faint and melancholy glimmer in the vast dark place, like glow-worms lost in space.

Mike looked at the men standing there, standing in silence, clad in rough leather clothes and skins of beasts, holding their wooden staves, fingering their beards. Mike looked and a great sadness came over him. So these were the Earthmen. And the books he had read, the Earth books? Where now was the glory they had described? Lost in war and death and decay and age; lost forever.

"Who brought me to this place?"

"I did," said a bearded giant half hidden in the dark, looming, a monstrous shape in the half-light.

The old man smiled. "Come with us. We will take you to our meeting place."

Mike walked with them in silence along the spectral hall of the shelter, not daring to speak, afraid to ask about Earth, afraid now to tell them how he had come.

The meeting place showed in the glimmer of firelight ahead. They descended the steps and Mike found himself in the midst of a throng of dark figures, all peering, whispering, pointing...

The old man took Mike's arm and they sat down on a rough wooden bench.

"Now, tell me—how did you come here? Where are you from? You speak the same language as we do, yet you are not of us. Your clothes are different, yet you are not one of the Others. Who are you?"

How could he tell these people? How could he say that he came from a twinkling point of light sixty-seven million miles away? How could he tell and expect to be believed?

"I have come from the sky."

"From the sky?" There was a muttering and a murmuring and a shifting of feet and a clattering of wooden staves.

"Yes, from the sky. But I am a friend." It was like the old books—the explorer landing among the primitive natives and trying to make himself understood. And these were the descendants of the Lords of the Universe who had sown their planet with cities and mighty railways and rocket ships, and had at length conquered the vast darkness of space itself.

"You say you are a friend, yet you come in a mighty machine that makes the night bright as day with flame."

How to tell these people? How to tell them?

There came a thin, quavering, dry old voice from the dark shadows. "You say you come from the sky?"

Mike turned and peered into the gloom. He saw the frail old woman crouching there like a spider with her legs, thin and withered, protruding from the rough cloak of leather.

"Yes, from the sky."

"I have heard tell that one day you might come." She turned to the old man. "It is true. He is a friend."

There came a murmuring from the people. They crowded closer but their voices were not angry. Mike had the feeling that this old woman had power over them. Perhaps she was the ruler. Her bleak little eyes glittered like tiny diamonds in the light of the wood fire; her old mouth worked soundlessly; her body shook with the effort of speech.

"I am free to go, then?" He hardly hoped they would say yes.

"You may do as you wish," said the old woman, smiling a slow, crackling smile. "You will find the way out along there." And a withered arm rose, shaking, and pointed to a narrow passage leading off the main hall.

Mike stood undecided. The passage led, presumably, out to the open and Kerry and Rennig and the ship. If he stayed here...

"Before I go will you tell me about this place?"

"What is there to tell? We live here; that is all."

"I am a stranger. I told you I came from—"

"From the *sky?*"

"Yes."

"What do you wish to know?" asked the old woman.

Mike sat down on one of the benches. "Everything," he said. "I want to know what it is like, living here. I want to know about this place, about the country, about your world."

And they told him.

They told him all that they knew. Told of the vast Abyss, glowing hotly and redly over the hills; told of the great cities, still dangerous, still full of the plagues and terrible radiations; told too of the Others—swarming over the planet, driving the true men to the vast underground shelters. Mike did not at first understand what these 'Others' were. Then, slowly, it came to him.

Mutants.

And the voices droned on and told him about them, about their deformities and their cruelty. And Mike found himself hating them, even as these last true men hated them.

"We are few now. There was a time when we were many. Once one of our band ventured into one of the smaller cities and found there many books telling of this world as it was a long, long time ago."

Mike leaned forward. "What happened to him? Where is he now?"

The old woman's eyes closed. "He returned here and showed us the books and it was only then that we realized where he had been."

"Yes—but what *happened?*"

"He brought the plague back with him. We killed him and burnt the books." Her voice shook and the thin claw hands quivered on her knees. "He was my son."

And so Mike learnt of these people and of their ways. He felt them cluster round him in the dark and tell him about themselves and he saw that at last they had accepted him.

The fire dimmed as they talked and one of the men heaped more wood on it from a pile in the corner of the hall. And the flames sputtered and roared and the wood glowed brightly, and someone brought bowls of fruit and some wine, and they sat and feasted and talked, Mike with them, Mike thinking: *And I must go, back to Rennig and Kerry, back to the scientific, emotionless remarks of the one and to the raucous blustering of the other, back to the ship, back!*

And here was *home*.

He was learning a lot about the people. He knew some of their names. The old woman was called Willa and the old man Gray. The man who had captured him and brought him here was Rik. Other names, too, flew through the conversation; names of all kinds all nationalities. Mike saw how mixed the gathering was, when he looked more closely. There were white and brown men and yellow and black men together, even as on Venus, even as he had read it was once on Earth, too.

"Tell me," he said, "where do the Others live? How many of them are there?"

The old woman Willa smiled. "Take a handful of sand and throw it in the air—can you count the grains as they fall?"

"There are as many as that?"

"There are as many. They have grown strong through the years, stronger than our people. They have bred like the beasts."

"Yes, but why do you have to fight with each other? Why can't you make some sort of truce, some sort of treaty?"

"Can you make peace with a wild beast that has been taught to hate you? No, we cannot make peace with them."

"But surely you can move away, then? Move where these Others cannot find you?"

"Move? But where? They are everywhere. We are only safe under the earth."

"Have you no better weapons than these clubs?"

"We have spears and swords, and bows and arrows."

"In my ship I have weapons. With *them* we can beat the Others."

"What sort of weapons?"

He searched through his mind for an answer that they would understand and could think of none. Then a word came to him. A word he had read in a child's book he had stolen from the vault. An *Earth* child's book.

"Magic weapons," said Mike.

"What are they?"

"I will bring them and you can see."

"You will return to your machine?"

"To my friends."

"Your friends?"

There was a rustle among them, a shuffling.

"Who are these friends? Are they like you?"

"Yes."

"Did they, too, come from the sky?"

"Yes. Yes, they did."

Silence while they thought about that. They looked at him closely as though to find whether he was speaking truthfully, as though by their piercing stares they could see through into his mind.

"Very well. Go and bring them here and bring these weapons also," said Willa.

"How do I get out of this place?"

Willa rose and pointed. "Down that corridor you will find a spiral stairway. That leads you out onto a hill. Go down the hill and turn to the south. Wait—I will send one of the men to guide you. Rik will go."

"He brought me here. He should know the way," smiled Mike. "Is that the only way out?"

"No. There is a passage leading to the white cliff, but the climb down is difficult."

"Well, I'll be going, then. I'll bring my friends back with me."

The man Rik stepped forward, leaning slightly on his staff.

Then Mike saw them.

They had been creeping along the side of the hall, in the darkness, in the gloom, away from the fire and the crowd of Earthmen.

Kerry and Rennig. Stepping softly, softly, with the glinting, evil, M.V. guns in their hands, their glare glasses pushed up on their foreheads now, their eyes piercing. Two beasts of prey about to make a kill...

Mike saw Kerry raise his gun.

"Don't. Kerry, *don't!*"

Mike pushed Rik swiftly to one side. Rik, taken off balance, half-turned, caught his foot on an uneven place on the floor and fell. The mist struck the wall in the same second that Mike heard the soft *ploof* of the gun. It struck and made solid that small space where Rik had stood.

"Stop it, Kerry. Don't shoot!" cried Mike again.

The block of solid death stood beside the wall. Rik crawled to his feet. The other Earthmen stood as though spellbound, as though frozen as Rik might so easily have been.

"Hold it! They're friendly!"

Kerry and Rennig approached cautiously, their guns still ready in their hands, their eyes still suspicious.

"Who are they, Mike?"

"They're Earthmen. It's all right." He turned to old Willa. "These are my friends—they thought I was in danger."

"Those are the weapons?"

"Yes."

She moved forward towards Kerry and held out her hand for the gun.

"Hey. Wait a minute—what is this? Mike, tell this old woman to keep her hands off!" The gun steadied in his hand. It pointed dangerously and his eyes became colder, harder. "Tell her, Mike!"

"Don't be a fool." Mike crossed swiftly and wrenched the gun from his hand with a sudden twist. *"There,"* he said, handing the weapon over to Willa. Kerry scowled and turned on Mike.

"Have you gone crazy?"

Rennig strode forward, now. He thrust his gun out to Willa and said: "Here!" The old woman took it and the others crowded closer.

Rennig edged close to Mike. "Have they harmed you?" he whispered.

"Of course not. They're friendly. They've been telling me all about themselves and this place. How on Earth did you find me?"

"We followed the tracks and then saw some smoke rising out of a hole in a cliff. We climbed the cliff and came through the cave."

"Then it's daytime?"

"Yes."

"Boy, I must have been unconscious for quite a while."

"What is this place?"

"It's one of the old raid shelters. They have to live here because they are constantly being attacked by mutants."

Rennig frowned. "Mutants?"

"Yes..."

At that moment old Willa stepped up, interrupting their conversation. She held the guns out to Mike and said: "I do not understand these things. But they are powerful and if you have more our people would be glad of them."

Mike smiled. "We have more," he said, ignoring the warning glances from Rennig and Kerry.

Then they all sat down again and the newcomers were told about Earth, as Mike had been told before them. And the fire was replenished and food and drink were brought again.

Rennig crouched nearer to old Willa and began to question her about the Abyss.

"You say it's always been there?"

"As long as I have lived it has been there, and as long as my father lived, and his father before him. It is as old as—as old as the World."

"No, Willa, not as old as the World. Not that old. There was a time when…"

And old Willa smiled and said: "I know. There was a time when there were people in the cities, when there were crops growing and hills green everywhere. There was a time when there were no Others. But that is past; too long past."

Mike leaned across. "That time might come back, Willa."

The old woman shook her head. "No, Mike. Not now."

Rennig said: "And these cities—what state are they in now? Can we go down to them?"

"No. The plague has made them too dangerous. None of our people go there now."

"But what are they *like*—the cities?"

"Big and silent. You can stand on the hill and look down on the near city and almost believe there are people there, or that the people will return in a second as though having only been away for a holiday. That is what the cities are like."

"But is all the world like this? Are there no cities left, no other Earthmen?"

Willa shrugged. "How can we tell? Our men have gone far in their travels and have always returned with the same story. It was like that in my father's time, too. Desolation everywhere. Everywhere the great silent cities and the dust and the bones of those who died."

"And the Others?"

"Yes, and the Others. They are everywhere now. They live in the forest's and fight amongst themselves and seek always to destroy us."

"But why? Why? Why do they want to kill you?"

The old woman closed her eyes. "Because we are human."

So it yet lived, thought Mike. So there still existed that spark of pride in the race, that spark the years and centuries of war and death and plague and horror had been unable to destroy. And Mike was glad.

And then old Willa told them how her family had ruled this band, had bound them together as a unit in the dim days long since passed away.

"My son strayed down into the city when still a boy. He brought back the books and we read them and realized where he had been and what he had done. He was too young to know."

Rennig looked at her sharply. "Too young to know what?"

"Too young to know why he should never have gone into the city. He might have brought the plague back to our people. He was killed."

"And the books?"

"Burned. Burned with his body."

Kerry broke in: "Tell me, how do you get food here?"

"On the hills there are many fruit trees. Mostly we eat fruit and sometimes a band of our men go out in search of wild animals. But we have to be so careful—the Others are everywhere—we cannot send many men for fear of being attacked while they are gone. And a small band might so easily be ambushed."

Kerry grunted and leaned back. Mike watched him out of the corner of his eye and saw him getting restless. Then he turned to talk to Willa and by the time he looked again Kerry was gone.

"Where's Kerry?"

Rennig glanced round. "Well, he was here a moment ago."

"Yes, but where is he *now?*"

Rennig grinned. "Does it matter? You're so touchy."

"No, I suppose it doesn't matter."

And they talked on, Willa telling them how they had guards posted at the entrance to the shelter to warn of the Others; telling how life went on under the earth so deep.

They prepared to turn in. Willa walked with them to a smaller chamber opening off the main hall where there were piles of skins and rugs stretched on rough wooden beds.

They stood talking and at that moment there came a scampering of feet, a muffled clatter of staves and voices raised in the still, silent air.

Willa turned. "What is that?"

'That' was Kerry. He was trundled up between two guards. "We caught him trying to escape."

Kerry struggled. "I was only going to look around—and who are you to start telling me what to do?"

Willa signed for them to let Kerry free. He stood there panting and scowling.

Willa said: "We are sorry this happened. Had you told us you wanted to go outside it would have been all right. The guards did not know you, you see."

"Well, I don't like it."

"We are sorry."

Kerry turned his back on the old woman. "Are we going back to the ship?"

Rennig said: "We've been invited to spend a while here."

He pointed at the small room.

"What *here?* What do you think I am—a worm? Listen, Rennig, I didn't come all this way to live underground I can tell you."

"Just for the moment, Kerry. Just for a while."

"Well, if you're both going to I suppose I'd better. Hey!" he shouted at one of the guards. "Bring us some more of that wine—and some fruit, too."

The guard turned questioningly to Willa who nodded.

Kerry smirked. "That's better," he said.

Mike glanced sideways at Willa as though to apologize, to make amends. The old woman's face was like a marble block, cut and worn by time, expressionless.

When Willa had retired Mike turned to Rennig and said: "How about going out and looking at the city tomorrow?"

Kerry laughed. "You're getting into the Earth ways already, talking of tomorrow like that as though it's night now—it's daylight still—the *afternoon.*"

"Well, I'm feeling too tired to go now. Let's make it tomorrow. I could do with a rest right now."

Rennig sat on one of the beds and said: "Me, too, all this excitement is bad for me."

Then the man came in with some bowls of fruit and some wine. He set them down on the table and went out, looking sourly at Kerry.

When he had gone Kerry said: "See that look he gave me? We're going to have trouble here if we're not careful."

"Well, *you* be careful, then," said Mike.

"What do you mean by that?"

"Just what I say. These aren't savages to be ordered about, Kerry. They're the last of the humans on this planet, so far as we know."

Kerry made a contemptuous sound. "Just because you've read all those books about Earth you've started to think Earthian. Why, just think what an opportunity we've got here. With our weapons we could wipe the floor with this bunch—and they know it. Think of it, Mike—from office clerk to king of a new planet! Sounds great, doesn't it?"

Mike stared at the floor.

"Why not? It's a great idea." Kerry gulped down some of the wine and filled his beaker again. "One thing I will say for these boys—they certainly know how to make good wine."

He gulped again.

"Well, I feel ready for some fun."

His voice rasped in the quietness, and the room, with its memories of Earthmen and of the doings of Earthmen, shuddered within itself. And Mike shuddered too.

Kerry stood up. "Well, now. That was good." He put the empty beaker down on the table and walked to the door. "Just going to stretch my limbs. Be seeing you."

And he was gone.

Mike and Rennig looked at each other in silence.

"We *are* going to have trouble, you know," said Rennig. Mike didn't answer him. He just sat and stared at the door and thought: *How he has changed. How different to the Kerry I knew back on Venus!* And he thought of the Earthmen and their quiet struggling against their enemies and of their life here on the dying planet. And the thoughts of Kerry and Rennig and Venus and the journey all faded away into the limbo of time lost, time forgotten.

CHAPTER TEN
City Silent, City Dead

The changing guard woke them and told them that morning had come. It was difficult to imagine it, down there so deep below the earth; difficult to think of dawn crawling up into the sky and the warm sun glimmering.

Old Willa came for them and they prepared to go out towards the hill where they could see the city.

Kerry strapped a needler to his belt. "Maybe we'll see something to eat. They say there are plenty of animals round these parts."

They went up the spiral staircase with Willa, Rik and three other Earthmen. It was a long climb and by the time they got to the top the old woman was exhausted. She sat down in the little guardhouse while one of the guards went for the rickshaw in which she traveled.

Rik pushed open the great metal door and the sunlight streamed in.

"Fine day," said Rik.

Kerry and Mike stepped outside and looked round. They were surrounded by piles of masonry and gutted, empty buildings overgrown now with weeds and creepers. The air was still and crisp.

Old Willa stepped into the rickshaw and they started off through the ruins towards a distant hill.

Turning, Willa said: "This must have been a small town once; the nearest city is over the hill. We can look down upon it."

Rennig looked at her questioningly. "Do the Others ever go into the city?"

"That we do not know. They live over in the forestland. We only see them when they raid our homes and sometimes our men see them when they are hunting."

"Are we likely to meet any?"

"We can never tell. They come silently and there are always so many of them. But you have your guns; they will not be able to face *them*."

To the west they saw a small herd of shaggy ponies grazing in the long grass; moving slowly off along the valley.

Kerry pointed to them and said: "There, Mike, just like in that book, horses, aren't they?"

"Yes. Horses, or ponies, rather."

They came out of the ruins and crawled slowly, slowly, up the hill, staring about them at the bleakness and the desolation. They saw a brown shaggy bear some way off, padding away into the forest. And they saw crows swirling in the sky and, once, a great eagle soaring over the hill.

Soon they were nearing the top of the hill and old Willa said:

"It is a strange sight, this city. I have never grown used to it, though I have been up here often. When you look down and see the great buildings standing there, some in ruins, some, the stronger ones, almost as fresh as when they were built, you find yourself thinking that the people must have all just gone off for a day's trip somewhere and must surely all return. But they will never return."

The sun climbed the heavens and the clouds that had been massing in the east started to spread outwards, bringing promise of rain.

Then they reached the top of the hill.

"There she is," said Willa.

And Rennig and Mike and Kerry stood looking down over the valley where the city lay like a child's model in the lemon light of day.

They did not speak for a moment; only stood and marveled and told themselves that this was no dream but reality.

The city was huge, spreading out into the distance. There were trees growing in the roads and the buildings were green with creeping weeds. Mike followed the great white road with his eyes, followed it past the huge office buildings, past the airport where, rusted and broken, there yet lay some rockets, fallen there like crumpled cigars tossed to the ground, useless, forgotten by time. And over the whole city there hung an air of waiting—as though, as Willa had said, the people would return at any minute, any second. The desolate emptiness they had expected was not there.

Mike felt a lump rising in his throat as he looked. *Here* is home, he thought. Here on Earth, here in this special place, among these people.

Kerry laughed. "Well, I wonder if anyone's at home." He threw back his great head and shouted: "Hullo, there!"

Silence save for the distant *caw* of a crow, flying high above them.

"Guess they're all on holiday!" Kerry strode off to the right of them and stood alone. And Mike thought: Soon something will happen between us. This cannot go on. Soon something *must* happen.

Willa pointed out the roads that stretched from the city like strands of some enormous spider's web. "Over there the road crosses a great river and goes on to another city almost as big as this one. Where we are standing there must have been houses at one time. All this land must once have been covered with buildings."

Then they turned to go back; Mike still seeing in his mind the city, not as it was, but as it must once have been, filled with people and roaring beetle cars, rockets blazing overhead, their trails of fire brightening the day. And he thought of the glory of Earth, a glory that now lay within the breasts of these last human beings.

On the return journey Kerry spotted a deer strolling with proud steps among the trees on a nearby knoll.

Both firing their needlers at once Rennig and Kerry brought the beast crashing down.

"Well, at least we'll have some decent food today," said Kerry. "That old animal ought to go a long way between the three of us."

Mike looked at him. "Between how many?"

"Three."

"Aren't you forgetting the others?"

"What others?"

"The other Earthmen. All food is shared out."

Kerry snorted. "We killed the damned thing. If this is the ways things are going I should think it's time we got back to the plane and took ourselves off. There's plenty more of this planet to see, you know."

The idea of leaving had never occurred to Mike. He stared with no little astonishment. "Leave here?"

"Why not? I want to *see* Earth now I've come all those million miles from home. There may be some sort of civilization on this planet—we can't tell. Just because the old woman says she's never heard tell of any more humans doesn't mean there aren't any."

They were a little behind the rickshaw and the Earthmen, then. Mike glanced ahead. "You mean you want to go now?"

Kerry grunted. "I don't know about *now*—what do you think, Rennig?"

"Well, if we stay a couple more days, that should be sufficient. I want to take the ship over the Abyss to see what it's like. And, as you say, we ought to see as much of Earth as we can."

Mike was silent. He knew that, logically speaking, they were both right. It would be stupid just to stay in this one place and live with these people. They had a space ship and therefore they could go wherever they pleased; therefore they *should* travel about and explore the planet. But the pull of the silent city was so great, so very, very powerful; and the thought of living with these people, too, was powerful. Mike knew what he ought to do and yet he knew also what he would do. He would stay. And he knew that the others would never consent to staying and would leave him.

They were almost through the belt of long grass when Rik called them to a halt and pointed towards the distant ruins where lay the entrance to the shelters.

"See there—movement."

They stared in the direction of the pointing finger. Kerry growled: "People—I can't see 'em."

"It is the *Others,*" said Willa softly. "They are attacking."

Mike pulled the needler from his belt. "Well, come on. We'll see what they think of *these.*"

Willa laid a hand on his arm. "Wait—it is no quarrel of yours. Go now to your machine. If you do not…"

"Nonsense. Of course it's my quarrel."

Rennig stepped forward. "She's right, Mike. It's no business of ours."

Mike smiled and said: "You, too, Rennig?"

The scientist went a little red. "What do you mean?"

"Never mind. Well, I'm going to help. You two do what you please." He saw them look at each other uneasily and then Rennig said:

"Well, all right, then—we'll help."

And they started off towards the ruins, their weapons ready in their hands.

CHAPTER ELEVEN
Battle

They left old Willa and her rickshaw hidden behind some low bushes. Two of the Earthmen stayed to guard her and Rennig left the M.V. fuel gun with one of them, after showing him how it worked. Then they stole up towards the ruins.

From a distance the Others looked little different from the ordinary Earthmen. But when you got nearer you could see.

Some of them were only mildly deformed; perhaps their ears were mere buttons protruding from a hairless skull, perhaps their noses were boneless, hanging in strange little bags in the center of their faces. But some were far worse. Some had twin heads, some were monsters in size, towering two and three feet above the tallest of the Earthmen, some were scaly and dwarfed. All were hideous.

Mike and the others heard the alarm bell clanging from the guardhouse: telling of the invading Others, warning the men below. Then the Others charged. They came across the ruined plateau in a straggling line, bearing clubs and spears, bows and arrows, rocks, weapons of all kinds. Their guttural shouts filled the still mid-morning air, frightening flocks of crows into rising, the sound biting into the cool, clear peace of the hills.

Mike brought his needler up and fired. They were hidden behind a crumbling wall on the flank of the invaders. They could see the arrows flying from the windows of the guardhouse, bringing the mutants down in ones and twos. Mike fired again and Rennig and Kerry joined him.

Under his breath Kerry said: "Why did you have to go and tell them we'd help for? We could have got away to the ship and left this damned place well alone. If only you'd kept your big mouth shut."

Mike picked off another mutant with his needler. "I said I'd help. There was no need for you to have stayed. You could have gone back to the ship with Rennig and left me here."

Kerry grunted something unintelligible and hunched himself beside the wall and peered round. "They're right up against the guardhouse now. Some of the Earthmen have come outside to fight; they're round the back of the guardhouse shooting with bows and arrows—what a mess to get mixed up in!"

"Stop grumbling, Kerry," said Rennig. "The thing is, now we've started, to find out how we can help best. We're not doing much good here."

"Well, what *can* we do?"

"I was just thinking—if we could get to the ship and bring back that crate of guns and take them to the guardhouse— why, we could finish this battle in a matter of minutes."

Kerry grinned wryly. "Sure we could. The thing is to get to the ship and back to the guardhouse without getting killed. If you know any easy way of doing *that*, do tell us."

Mike said: "I'll go."

"Well, the sooner you start the better," said Kerry.

Mike nodded. "Let's see—the ship's somewhere over there, isn't it? If I can get away into the valley without the mutants seeing me I should be able to make it fairly easily. You can keep me covered while I run for it."

He stood up, thrust his needler into his belt and ran. They watched him as he darted from ruin to ruin, from one pile of rocks to another, from one gutted building to the next. Then he was gone.

The Others seemed too taken up with their attack to notice anything that was happening behind them. They had massed around the guardhouse and were shouting and waving their weapons.

"How is he going to get that crate of guns back here? It's as heavy as hell," said Kerry.

Rennig smiled. "What I'm wondering about is how he's going to get it through to the Earthmen!"

"Well, he got us all into this mess; it's his funeral."

"That doesn't make the problem any easier. *Look out!*" The two Others had approached silently while the men were talking, had crept up with their spears ready, had come like beasts, fangs bared.

Kerry fired twice and the first mutant fell in a smoking pile; Kerry had used full power. The second one stepped back and screamed at the sight. Rennig shot him in the stomach and he fell forward, sprawling, sagging.

Rennig smiled. "Good shooting."

"Not so good if any of the others noticed it. We should make a pretty target here."

Rik and the two other Earthmen who had been crouching beside the wall some few yards off crept closer. Rik said: "It looks as though they are going to retreat. They are breaking up and coming this way. We'd better get out of here."

"Where to? I can't see anywhere to hide."

Rik pointed across to a nearby ruin. "There's a cellar in that building; goes quite deeply underground. We could try there."

"Well, anything's better than staying and getting killed. Come on."

They stood up and, casting frequent glances over their shoulders, made for the old building. They saw the mutants breaking into smaller groups, coming away from the guardhouse like flies suddenly leaving food. The Earthmen inside were still filling the air with arrows and the bodies of the Others lay piled about like stuffed dolls thrown carelessly down by a petulant child. And the crows, tired now of circling the battleground, started downward, wheeling and cawing and wheeling again, came to settle and devour.

Rennig followed the others into the ruined building, cast a last glance behind him and tucked his needler into his belt. Rik pointed to the steps of the cellar and they went down.

"Mike won't know where to look for us," said Kerry. "One of us had better stay near the surface and watch for him."

"I will stay," said Rik.

"Then you'd better take this," said Rennig, handing him his needler. "All you do is point it and squeeze this little thing underneath."

Rik took the gun, nodded and braced himself on the steps. The others went down.

After Mike had left the ruins he ran some hundred-odd yards down the slope into what looked like a valley. In actual fact it was a crater made some centuries past by the explosion of an atomic bomb. He ran over the soft red sand among the scrubby bushes, ran hearing the cries and noises of the battle grow fainter behind him, ran knowing the future of the battle might well lie in his hands. The problem of getting the guns in to the Earthmen was running through his mind and it was this that made him careless.

He ran out of the scrub and started to climb over a fallen tree and then he saw them.

There were three—one, leading, a giant some seven or eight feet tall, the others both in some way deformed.

He pulled his needler from his belt in the same second that the giant raised his spear and threw it. Mike jerked himself to one side, fell and fired. The shot went wide. He fired again and the giant uttered a little gasping sound and collapsed. The two other mutants backed away in terror. Mike shot them without rising from the ground. Then, slowly, carefully, he raised himself up. But there were no more mutants in sight. Those three had probably fallen behind in the first attack.

Mike put his gun away again and continued. He now had some idea of his whereabouts and in a little while he saw the gleaming pencil of the ship sparkling in the sun about a quarter of a mile away.

The aluminum tents were still standing and the ashes of their fire were undisturbed. Apparently the mutants had not seen the ship—or, if they had seen it, were too afraid to approach closely. Mike went up the ladder and into the ship.

He sat down on one of the seats to get his breath back, then he went into the store and brought the crate of guns up into the control cabin. He looked inside.

The guns were all there—sparkling and deadly. There were six needlers and six electronic rifles and at the bottom of the crate he found one of the new Bygrave Burners. He smiled and spoke softly to himself: 'Boy! With that we shan't have to get the guns into the Earthmen. We can do the whole thing from outside. These Burners are really the goods. With this one alone I could bring those mutants down like flies off a wall.'

He lugged the crate to the door of the ship. 'I'll never get this lot back in time. The best thing would be to just take the Burner—I can do enough damage with that on my own.'

He hoisted the weapon on to his shoulder and started down the ladder to the ground. The Burner was no lightweight and by the time he had reached the bodies of the three Others he had killed he was breathing hard and stumbling, too.

The crows cawed distantly; the sun moved slowly in the sky; rain clouds that had been gathering all day crept together now, with the wind that had sprung up and was now whining through the grasses. There was a listlessness about the day, a sullenness.

Mike walked up the slope and stopped behind a tall tree. He looked over and saw the mutants gathered into groups, pointing, talking. He heard their voices harshly chattering, saw the last of the sunlight glint on their spearheads. Then the clouds cuddled and smothered the sun, and the wind strengthened and the first few drops of rain started to fall.

Mike looked up at the tree. I can get up there, he thought; I can climb up there with the Burner, set it up on that branch and cover the lot of them. It's perfect.

He hitched the Burner farther up on his shoulder and started to climb the tree. Still—none of the mutants had noticed him. He reached a thick branch some twelve feet from the ground and straddled it, lowering the Burner in front of him so that it rested on the wood, its nose pointing towards the battleground.

Then the wind, strengthening, brought the rain from the clouds in sheets of bitter drops, biting through the trees, slashing, cutting. Mike felt the rain on his face as he adjusted the range of the Burner. The muzzle pointed directly towards the mutants who were grouped about a ruined tower on the extreme edge of the plateau.

Then he remembered that Kerry and Rennig and the Earthmen were hiding somewhere in that direction. 'Hell, I'd better start from the other side and trust to luck they haven't moved.'

He turned the Burner again, readjusted the range and switched over to 'Continuous Fire.'

Then he pressed the contact switch and squeezed the trigger.

The flame came out a pale blue, changing to red as the beam lengthened. It swept the ground and the sharp smell of burning filled the air. Then it hit the mutants.

Now the Burners are supposed to be used for clearing areas of grass and bushes, but they make very efficient weapons just the same.

The flame licked amongst the Others with the sound of paper crackling. And the blackened, scorched and smoking bodies dropped one by one as the heat wrapped round them and passed on. Their screams ripped into the air and Mike winced as he heard them.

There was nothing they could do. Some tried to run but the flame got them before they reached the edge of the plateau and they fell, giant and dwarf together.

When the flame hit one of the crumbling heaps of masonry or perhaps a ruined building there was a sharper crackling as the stone crunched and the steel melted and the wood and plastic burst into flame. And the trees took fire and fell; and the dry, brown grass that grew everywhere became a mass of flames, cutting off the mutants' retreat.

Only a very few managed to escape. They were the ones who, having escaped the beam, ran straight through the flaming grass and disappeared, their hair and clothes aflame, into the trees on the other side of the ruins.

And the rain fell steadily down, making the flaming grass belch up clouds of thick smoke which, caught by the hurrying, whining wind, came across the plateau in tortuous billows, writhing and curling in fantastic shapes, making Mike cough and his eyes water.

Slowly, slowly, he came down from the tree with the Burner, inactive, silent, still clutched tightly in his hand. He leaned against the tree and retched, thinking of the burning, blackened shapes he soon would have to see.

Then he started up towards the plateau.

When the mutants started to retreat from the guardhouse Rennig and Kerry and the Earthmen had frozen in the darkness of the cellar, making themselves a part of the shadows there, pressing closely against the walls. And they saw the Others' shadows blot out the light that filtered down into the cellar and they breathed softly and the sweat began to run on their foreheads.

Then the shadows passed and they heard the guttural voices softly murmuring above.

Then came the screaming.

It was Rennig who realized first what was happening. "It's Mike—he's using the Burner. I bet that's what it is. He's using the Burner!"

"What burner?" whispered Kerry.

"The Bygrave Burner I brought at the bottom of that crate of needlers and electronic rifles. I'd forgotten all about the damned thing—and old Mike's found it. Listen to that screaming!"

There was no need to listen very hard. The screams came to them harshly, there in the cellar. And soon the smoke, too, came down to them.

There was no need to listen nor was there need to see; they could imagine all that was happening. Rennig pressed his face against the wall of the cellar and closed his eyes, seeing in his mind the blackened bodies falling, unable to remember that these creatures were little better than beasts, remembering only that they walked on two legs and were descended from beings like himself.

Then they heard the trampling of feet as the mutants tried to get away, heard the screams get louder as the tortured, flaming creatures ran in mad attempts to escape.

Then the screams died and the smoke increased in volume as the rain grew heavier.

Then there was a long silence.

"It's over," breathed Kerry. "Let's go up."

They walked slowly up the steps and peered out into the rain and the smoke. They could see little—everywhere the smoke blew in great solid walls and everywhere was the pungent smell of burning.

They fought their way through the smoke towards the place where they had left old Willa and the Earthman guard. They found them crouched behind the rickshaw. The old woman's eyes gleamed when she saw them.

"I saw it all," she said. "I saw the flame come down from the trees across the plateau; saw it cut through the Others like a great sharp knife. Which one of you did it?"

Rennig smiled. "It was Mike—the one you captured. He brought the weapon from our ship. We were hidden in the cellar of one of the buildings and did not see it."

Her dry old face screwed up with the smoke blowing against it. "I have never seen such death. You must have passed the bodies without noticing them in the smoke. But I saw the ground, before the grass caught fire; it was *black* with them, black with burning and with death."

They helped the old woman to her feet and one of the Earthmen dragged the rickshaw upright and in she climbed. "Let us get back to the guardhouse. There will be many men wounded who will need care."

Rennig said: "We had best go and look for Mike. The smoke is blowing right across to where he must have been. He may get lost if he starts off for the guardhouse in this. That smoke is enough to blind anyone when it's blowing right in your eyes."

Willa nodded. "Yes. Go and find him and bring him to me." Then the Earthman gripped the shafts of the rickshaw and she was gone into the smoke, leaving Kerry and Rennig alone.

"Hey—did you hear that?" said Kerry. "She said, 'Go and find him,' as if we were servants or something!"

Rennig smiled stonily. "Never mind. We'll be out of this place soon."

"With Mike feeling the way he does about it all?"

"Yes."

"He won't like it."

"He'll have to like it."

"Of *course* he will, Rennig!"

Rennig turned and looked into the smoke. "Come on—let's find him. We've got to bring the hero in for her ladyship's blessing."

When they reached him the smoke had thinned and the rain had gentled a little, lulling now in a soft drizzle, making a grayish haze among the trees.

Mike was huddled at the foot of the slope. They undid his collar and Kerry rubbed some wet grasses over his forehead to bring him to. He shook himself and sat up.

"Kerry..."

"It's all over now. You killed 'em all, remember? The battle is won and you're the hero. Satisfied?"

Mike turned and struggled to his feet, swaying there unsteadily, gazing out at the smoky plateau, imagining again the licking flame, the falling, blackened bodies.

"It's finished?"

"Yes. All finished." Kerry laughed. "There's only the clearing-up left to be done."

Then he saw Mike's strained white face and he didn't say any more. They made their way across to the plateau and began to walk towards the guardhouse, coughing as the smoke wreathed about them, carefully avoiding the sinister black heaps that lay scattered here and there like tumbled toy soldiers burnt and blistered over a gas jet.

The Earthmen were pouring out of the guardhouse now, cheering and shouting, throwing high their spears, roaring their delight through the smoke and the mist.

Mike and the others pushed their way through them towards the guardhouse but hardly had they gone a dozen steps through the dense crowd when the word went round that these men had saved the underground village from pillage and disaster, that they were heroes with magic weapons who had come from the sky to help in the great battle against the Others.

And three hefty Earthmen converged on each of them, lifting them shoulder high, carrying them in a boisterous, cheering line towards the entrance to the shelters. Round and round milled the Earthmen, cheering and shouting and banging their weapons together.

At last Mike and his friends managed to free themselves and went into the guardhouse and down the spiral staircase to where the wounded were lying, the womenfolk hurrying amongst them with bowls of water to wash the wounds, with bandages, with food and drink. And old Willa was there, sitting on a low bench talking to Gray and one or two of the elders. She looked up when she saw Mike and smiled.

"So you are safe?"

"Yes."

"We are greatly in your debt. But for your help the Others would have broken into the guardhouse and might easily have beaten us altogether."

Mike shrugged: "I did what I could."

She smiled again. "You did well. Rest now and refresh yourselves." She signed to one of the Earthmen who went away and returned with some fruit and wine.

None had eaten since early that morning and they fell on the food ravenously. Kerry refilled his beaker with the strong red wine. "What happened to that deer I killed? I'd clean forgotten it in all the excitement."

"I sent one of my men to fetch it. It is being roasted at the moment. If you go down to the main hall you can see it."

Kerry gulped down his wine and stood up. "I think I will, too. I'm just dying to see that creature ready to eat." He walked off between the two lines of wounded, away in the torchlight towards the main hall.

Up above the Earthmen were dragging the bodies of the Others towards the center of the plateau. Some of the men had collected a great pile of brushwood and grass and others were piling the bodies on top in readiness for the great burning. The smoke had cleared and the grass was just smoldering in patches, still giving off the sharp, pungent smell. But the mist was strengthening, taking the place of the clouds of dense smoke, obscuring again the view of the distant hills.

Then they set fire to the wood.

It burned slowly at first; then, as the drier wood caught, the flames started to lick round the piled bodies on the top.

The Earthmen stood back and cheered again and again as the smoke mingled with the mist and as the sharp crackling snapped out over the ruins, borne by the wind across to them. It was a harsh sound, a satisfying sound.

Below Kerry watched the great deer being roasted on the spit as he drank down beaker after beaker of the rich red wine. After a while Rennig and Mike came to join him; Rennig thinking of the morrow when they would all be away from these underground shelters, away and roaring in the ship above the planet, exploring, searching, recording. And Mike was thinking of the morrow, too; knowing that the others would want to leave, knowing that *he* would want to stay.

Kerry made things worse for him by saying: "Oh, boy! It looks good! Think they'll let us take some away with us when we go tomorrow? It'd make a change from those capsules."

Rennig nodded. "I should think they would. We're the heroes, remember?"

And Kerry laughed.

CHAPTER TWELVE
Of Venus or of Earth?

The next morning Mike was awakened by the heavy tread of the changing guard. He blinked, shook his head and rolled over on the pile of furs. He sat up.

Rennig was still sleeping in the corner and Kerry was lying half across his bed, snoring loudly. There was a small pile of metal wine jugs on the floor beside him—all empty.

Mike rose and stretched and started to dress. The sight of Kerry lying there made him want to get out into the open air as quickly as possible. He stuck a needler into his belt and walked softly from the room and along the passage to the spiral staircase.

Many of the Earthmen were awake and on the move already, and they smiled as they saw him, smiled and remembered the previous day, remembered that this was the man who had destroyed the Others.

Up the stairs he went, flight after twisting flight, until he reached the guardhouse. Again the smiles, the remembering written on the faces.

He went out on to the plateau and looked about.

Where the funeral pyre had been there was now a pile of grayish ashes, blown here and there by the wind, caught in sudden little furtive whirlwinds, sent scurrying into the ruined buildings racing across the dead land, spreading news of the burning, of the strange and terrible flame that had licked out of the forest and destroyed the attackers.

Mike made his way across the plateau and started in the direction of the hill that overlooked the city. He walked quickly, quite sure of himself, feeling so very much at home.

He climbed the hill and felt the wind blow against his face, watched the birds circling high up against the blue, heard their voices in the morning air, and the feeling of contentment deepened, strengthened, as he reached the top of the hill and walked to where he could look down and see the city spread out under his eyes.

It had not changed, of course. It was still as silent, still as ruined, still waiting for the people to return, still watching for them.

Mike breathed in the fresh air of Earth, looked about him in the cool morning. 'I'm staying,' he whispered to the hills and the sky and the silent city.

'I'm staying and the others can do what they like. They can take that rocket ship off anywhere they please—*anywhere,* but I'm staying.'

He stayed for quite a while, gazing down and dreaming of the city as once it must have been and seeing it as it might yet be, perhaps a hundred years hence, perhaps a thousand.

Then he turned and walked off down the hill, turning away from the plateau and making towards the ship.

'I'll get back now and collect my things. Take them back to the shelter before Kerry or Rennig gets wise to what I'm going to do. Then I can just tell them I'm not going off with them.'

He walked more quickly, hurrying through the brown scrub, heedless now of the birds singing, of the wind blowing against him; wanting only now to make the break with the past, to finish with Rennig and Kerry, finish and forget. And somewhere in his mind a small, soft voice kept telling him that it would not be as easy as all that, telling him that something was going to happen. Something very nasty...

He came through the trees that bordered the place where the ship stood, gleaming and strange in the sun.

The door was open and the ladder still clung to the side.

Mike looked curiously at the tents, flattened down, ripped as though by mighty hands, the aluminum fiber cracked and torn and buckled, the ashes of their small fire scattered.

He started to climb the ladder slowly, his needler in his hand, peering cautiously upwards at the dark hole of the open door.

There came no sound from inside, no sound at all yet Mike *felt* that there was someone or something in there...

He put one hand up to the door and raised himself silently, needler pointed, breath held.

Then a voice said: "Oh—it's *you!*"

It was Rennig, standing in the shadows with a needler in his hand. He put the weapon in his belt and came forward, helped Mike inside. "What were you doing there? I thought it was one of the mutants."

Mike straightened up. "*I* thought there was a mutant inside *here*. I saw the tents all knocked down and I came up to see what had happened." He looked at Rennig more closely and saw the white strained face, the tight, working, muscles of the jaws, saw the angry glinting in his eyes.

"What *has* happened?"

"Plenty."

"Yes, but *what?*"

Rennig pointed upwards to the control cabin. "Let's go up."

They climbed up the ladder, Rennig in the lead, Mike following, puzzled, trying to imagine what was wrong.

In the cabin Rennig stood up and indicated the room with a quick, angry wave of his hand. "See?"

Then Mike saw.

Someone or *something* had been in the cabin and had done their best to wreck it. The intricate controls by the vision screen were smashed and tangled; coils of wire issued from the buckled gauge cases and fell like metal spaghetti on to the steel floor of the cabin.

"What happened?" asked Mike.

Rennig shook his head. "I can only guess. I should say one of the Others got in here. You must have left the ladder down and the door unlocked when you fetched the Burner yesterday."

Mike nodded. "Yes—come to think of it I believe I did. But what's actually *wrong*? I mean—does the ship still run?"

"There's only one thing that's broken beyond all repair, that's the Automatic Control. The other things really only need a couple of hours work, in spite of the way they look. But that Automatic Control..."

"Gone?"

"Absolutely gone."

"No hope of repairing it?"

"None. If we were back on Venus in the laboratory it would take me a month or so, probably. Out here there isn't a chance. I've only got a small repair kit and we didn't bring many spares because of the weight."

He walked across to the vision screen and pointed to the intricate machine beside it; the machine that had clucked and clacked and guided the three of them across sixty-seven million miles of space. Bits of the machine were still intact but most was spilled out on the floor in a slag-heap of broken valves, coiling wires, smashed dials, tubes, couplings, lenses, condensers; everything spilled out and most of it smashed beyond recognition.

"Sorry to be dumb, Rennig, but surely your spares would cover this? I mean, all these things here look like ordinary bits of apparatus to me—can't you rig *something* up?"

"No."

"Well then, what does it mean? Is the Automatic essential for running the thing?"

"Of course not. It just means that we shall all have to learn a bit more about the plane and be prepared to do some work when we take off and when we land. Otherwise things aren't as bad as they look."

Mike looked away quickly, seeing that now was his chance to speak, to tell Rennig that he wasn't going. But the scientist had moved across the room and was bending beside the tangled wires tumbling from a gash in one of the controls.

"This can soon be put right, Mike—can you go down to the store and get the repair kit?"

Mike went from the cabin and climbed down into the store and began looking for the small repair box. And he thought:

How shall I tell him that I am not returning? After this time together, after he has brought me here to Earth, after he rescued me from the green room back on Venus, how shall I tell him?

He went back up with the repair kit and put it on the floor. "Oh—Rennig..."

"Uh-huh?"—taking up the kit and opening it.

"I've been thinking."

"Yes? Hand me that valve, will you?"

"This one?"

"That's it. Thanks. Well?"

"Now I've been with these people for a while I've got to like them. It's funny, you know. I feel so much more at home here, somehow."

Rennig knelt in front of the control box so that Mike could not see his face. "It's quite natural. You thought about Earth so much, that's the trouble. You'll forget about it all once we're away."

Then Mike saw the end of a heavy spanner sticking from under a pile of charts on Rennig's desk—a spanner bent and scarred and scratched. Mike looked at it more closely as Rennig bent over the control box. The scratches were *new*.

Slowly it came to him. He saw the plan that must have formed in the scientist's mind, a plan to make sure that he went with them when they left. Rennig had returned here early in the morning and had done all this damage himself, purposely smashing only things that could be repaired quickly—except for the Automatic Control, though probably even that was still really in working order. Rennig would then count on his being willing to stay with them to work the ship manually.

"You planned it all very well, didn't you, Rennig?"

"Eh?" The thin head turned from the control box and the cold gray eyes slitted and stared. "What was that?"

"I said you planned it all very well. All this damage. Everything."

The scientist put the valve he had been holding down on the floor and stood up. "What's gone *wrong* with you? Are you ill?"

Mike smiled. "No. No, I'm not ill at all. I've just tumbled to it all, your little plan for keeping me with you." He pulled the spanner out from under the charts and papers. "You must have had quite a time, smashing all these things up."

Rennig said nothing. His mouth drew up into a long thin line and the muscles started to work along his cheeks. Then he smiled, abruptly, splitting his face, showing gleaming teeth. "So you saw through it, eh?"

"Yes."

"Well, can you blame me? I thought you might want to stay in this place and I thought it would be better if you didn't."

"Better for me, or for you and Kerry?"

"Better for all of us." He started to walk about the small cabin, his eyes glittering, his face moving; Mike was still, waiting to hear his words.

"It's all very well to say you like living here now, but what about after a few years of living underground? It won't be so pleasant then, you know. You've got to admit it, Mike, these people are a lot different to the Earthmen of the days of your books. They're not much better than savages, really."

The sound of the birds singing in the trees came through from outside. To hear them you had to strain your ears.

Rennig came and put a hand on his arm. "I'm not just thinking of the ship, Mike, when I say I want you to come with us. I know what's best for the three of us. We came here to find out what the planet is like. I don't know the reasons you and Kerry had for wanting to know that—but mine was a very special one."

Mike drew his mind away from where it had been lingering, on the hill overlooking the dead city, among the trees and birds and the blue skies of Earth. "What special reason was that?"

The scientist switched on the vision screen and they looked and saw the waving treetops and the distant hills and the plateau and, so far away, the guardhouse above the shelters.

"See all that? That's a new planet, Mike. I know it's dying and probably a good bit of it is radioactive. I know all that— but it's still land. And there's nothing Venus wants as much as new land. Think of it—a whole new world as big as ours ready for the plucking!"

Mike frowned uncomprehendingly. "What *are* you talking about?"

"This place Earth, of course. Now tell me—what is it that stops the Venusians from spreading out and filling their entire planet?"

"The fact that Venus has a Night Side and a Day Side, the first is too cold and the other too hot."

"Exactly. Only the Twilight belt can support life. And here we have a world with conditions infinitely better than those of our own Twilight Zone, and a world with only mutant freaks and a handful of barbarians as inhabitants." He spread his hands in the air; showing with a gesture how easy it all was, how simple.

"And you're suggesting *Venusians* come here, come to Earth?"

"Why not?"

And then Mike seemed to see the hills greener, the skies bluer, the birds' songs louder, the land more inviting, more homely. "Why not? Because for one thing we'd get imprisoned and sentenced to the green room as soon as we set foot on Venus again."

"Ah—but we wouldn't come down and land in the middle of First Highway. We'd come down on the Day Side or the Night Side. Then we'd hide the ship and get back to First City."

"And then—? Aren't you forgetting that space travel is forbidden? And besides, I couldn't show my face anywhere; I've been condemned to the green room once. They wouldn't bother to find out where I'd been at all. They'd get rid of me mighty quickly."

Rennig sat on the edge of his desk and looked at Mike long and hard. "Now, listen to this," he said. "I know what I'm talking about. The Rulers know all about Earth, but they are the *only* ones who do. If I went to the heads of several Venusian companies I know—they would back me in sending an expedition here. If I turned up and showed them a carefully constructed and detailed map of the entire planet, pointing out the possibilities of colonization—why, they'd be falling on my neck and *begging* me to take them there and set up a Venusian colony."

"And the Rulers? What about the laws against space travel?"

"There are a good many people on Venus who are pretty sick of being told what to do, especially the scientists. I'd back a million credits to one we'd have a "bloodless revolution" on our hands before we'd finished."

"No."

Rennig's smile dropped like a mask falling. You could almost hear it hit the metal floor. "What do you mean, no?"

"No, I won't do it and you're not going to try it, either!"

"Now, come off it, Mike. Don't get sore." The eyes glinted, the muscles worked along his cheek. "And above all don't start telling me what to do!"

Mike saw them coming, in his mind, saw the space ships full of the Venusians trailing down through space to the small, sad, dying planet; saw the ships open and belch forth clouds of the colonists who would raze the plague-filled city, would fill in the vast dark shelters, would burn up the mutants and the Earthmen alike and drive the beasts away into the forests. And when he looked closely at their faces he saw that they were all either Rennig or Kerry. And the Rennigs plotted plots of conquest on this planet, and the Kerrys shouted and drank and blustered and made fun of the Earthmen and their ways.

The creeping smile returned to Rennig's mouth: "Let's forget the arguments, huh? We'll stay here another day and we can sleep on it. You'll feel better tomorrow."

"I feel fine now."

"Well, I don't want to argue any more. Let's get back to the shelter, shall we?"

Mike made no move to go. He leaned against the wall of the cabin and watched the scientist and he thought, as always: This is home, here. And he wants to take me from it and then return with more and more Venusians and make this place a new colony, filled with men who know nothing of Earth and its history, know nothing of its traditions and its past. They will kill the Earthmen and they will burn the cities and set up new ones. And then Earth will really be a dead world.

"Coming?"

Mike rested his hand easily on the needler in his belt. "Did you mean what you were saying just now? About returning to Venus, about bringing Venusians here?"

"Certainly I did. But we'll talk about it later, shall we?"

"I want to talk about it now."

"Oh, come on! You're all worked up about it. Let's leave it."

Mike picked up the heavy spanner. "No, Rennig. *Now.*" He walked across to one of the great control panels. "I'm going to finish what you started."

Rennig darted forward. "You can't do that. You can't break up the ship! I have no welding apparatus here to repair it...!"

Mike smiled slowly and brought the spanner down with a crunch against the row of valves. "You weren't meant to be able to repair anything. You're not leaving."

Again the spanner rose and fell, again and again. Mike's eyes gleamed brightly as he destroyed the valves and the switches and the wires and all the other things that made the ship run, made it spaceworthy.

The voice came from behind him, soft, sure, deadly.

"Put that spanner down."

He turned slightly, seeing the needler in Rennig's hand, seeing also the cruel stare, the fingers white against the trigger.

"Put that spanner down and stand over against the wall."

Mike did not move. "Don't be a fool, Rennig. Put that needler away."

"No, Mike." The needler steadied. It was pointing at his stomach.

Mike moved then; moved like a cat sideways and caught Rennig's wrist even as his finger tightened on the trigger. A livid stream of fire burnt a gash in the wall. There was a smell of burning.

They wrestled in silence, swaying together, veins standing out in bunches on their foreheads. Then Mike wrenched away and got an arm under Rennig's chin, still holding the wrist that grasped the needler. He started to propel the scientist across the floor.

Neither of them saw the small valve lying there. It had spilled out from one of the controls and had remained, miraculously, intact.

It exploded with a sharp *plop* beneath their feet. Both jerked together and they fell.

On the floor Mike heard the tiny sound of the needler before he felt the body jerk beneath him, felt the heat against him and smelt the raw smell before he realized what had happened.

He straightened up slowly. Rennig was lying very still at his feet. *Very* still.

He turned him over gently with his foot and then, after seeing, he retched.

The needler, touched off by the jolt of falling, had done a good job on the scientist's face. There wasn't much left of it.

The small burning smell lingered in the cabin.

Mike looked away.

Funnily the sick feeling he had had was gone. He stood there quite steady and cool now. He didn't look at Rennig as he walked to the trap door of the cabin and climbed down the ladder to the main door. He paused and looked out and breathed in the fresh earthy smell of the trees.

Then he climbed the outside ladder down to Earth.

CHAPTER THIRTEEN
Another Man Dies

The purpose in his step was no longer there. He walked dreamily, his eyes seeing nothing but Rennig's raw, blackened face and staring eyes, and the smell of burning lingered still in his nostrils.

He did not return to the city but turned west towards the plateau, his feet making soft, quick, sighing sounds on the grass of the slope. The sun shone beamingly, cheerfully. It was a lovely day.

In the distance there were two figures and Mike, unseeing, walked on towards them.

It was as though there were two people there in his mind, two Mikes, both arguing together. And one was saying: 'It was an accident. Of course you did the right thing. Remember old Willa? Didn't she let her son, her own *son*, be burned because there was danger to the race, to Earth? And aren't *you* really of Earth? Of course you did right; Rennig wanted this world overrun with Venusians, he wanted to see Earth just a Venusian colony. He had to be stopped. And the other Mike would reply: 'How could you have done it? Rennig and Kerry saved you from the green room and brought you here to Earth. Without Rennig there would have been no space ship and no voyage. But for him you would still be working in the First Library back on Venus. And in spite of all these things you fought with him and he died.'

The figures drew nearer. Mike suddenly saw them emerge from the blur of memories sailing like gray and purple clouds before his eyes.

"Gray, Rik, what is it?"

The two Earthmen's faces were troubled. They looked at each other, each waiting for the other to speak first.

"Well—what has happened?"

"It's difficult," began Rik.

"We thought," started Gray.

They both stopped and looked at each other again. Then Gray said: "It's this. We are very grateful for what you did for our people yesterday, and we wondered whether you and your friends will be staying long with us."

The words had tumbled over each other coming out. They swirled in Mike's mind like tadpoles in a glass jar. He couldn't seem to catch them, to understand. He said: "Well, it depends—I would like to stay for some time."

The old man's lips worked. "And your friends?"

"What about my friends? I don't think they'll be staying."

The Earthmen looked at each other again and Mike saw relief in their glances.

"Why? What's wrong?"

"It's the man you know as Kerry."

"So?" This was it, thought Mike. He'd done something this time. And then he thought again. Why should he worry about what Kerry did? Kerry was a Venusian—he was an Earth man.

"That is what we came to tell you. One of the guards saw you go in the direction of your machine and we came to tell you."

"Tell me what?"

"Your friend—he has drunk too much of the wine. He is dangerous. The people are afraid of him."

"Where is he?"

"Down in the main hall. He has one of those guns. The people are afraid."

Mike nodded and the dreaminess went from his eyes. "I'll do what I can," he said. And they went towards the plateau, walking softly through the grass together, with the fresh morning air about them.

It was such a long, long way down the spiral stairs to the corridors and the halls. Mike listened to the echoing clang of his boots on the metal stairs. The two Earthmen were in front, both carrying rush torches which burned feebly and made flickering shadows dance upon the stairs and on the tall stone walls.

When they reached the corridor Mike said: "Okay, I'll go on and see him now. You say he's in the main hall?"

"He was when we left him. Your other friend left early this morning but this Kerry, he started to drink wine as soon as he woke."

"I'll see what I can do." And he was walking away from them, his hand resting uneasily on the needler in his belt.

Kerry was sitting on one of the wooden benches beside the fire. Mike heard his voice, raised and hollow in the vast hall. "Come on, get some more wood for this fire, can't you?" He swayed on the bench and reached out for the metal wine jug and the empty beaker. Then he saw Mike.

"Well, hullo there. *Mike* of all people. Come and have a drink. There's plenty left." He tilted the jug to prove it and some of the rich red wine slopped out on to the floor and formed a small puddle. "What happened to you all morning? I've been waiting for you—thought you might like to join me in a little celebration before we leave."

Mike stood cold and hard and still beside the fire. "No, thanks, Kerry."

"Well, I just thought I'd ask. Never can tell." He filled the beaker. "Tell you what, have you had a look at some of the girls they've got down here? I've had 'em all running round me today. All you got to do is wave a needler about the place and they're yours. Fact." To demonstrate he pulled his needler from his belt and waved it. Nobody ran round him. Then he glared across the fire and squinted. Something moved in the shadows.

"Come on, round here by me, unless you want to get your head burnt up."

A piece of the darkness detached itself, became lighter as it drew nearer and emerged a girl. She stood by the side of the fire, her face a stone mask in the flickering light.

"See what I mean?" said Kerry thickly.

"That's Rik's woman, Kerry," said Mike softly.

"Who the hell's Rik?"

"The man who brought me here."

"*Man?* You call him a man! These creatures are more like apes; a sort of cross between one of those apes and a Venusian sand dog." He belched.

"Come on, Kerry."

"Come on where?"

"Back to the ship."

"What for?"

"Rennig's there. He's waiting for us. He sent me to find you."

Kerry's face coiled up in a scowl. "Sent you to find me, did he? I'm not going to be brought here and taken there just when he pleases. Still, if we're going to leave I suppose I'd better come. Is that it, eh? Are we going to leave?"

Mike nodded quickly, not looking at him. "That's right, we're going to leave."

Kerry grunted and struggled to his feet. He swayed slightly and held on to the bench as he straightened up. Then he was sick on the floor.

Mike waited a while and then took his arm. "Come on, this way out, old man." Together they left the hall and as they did so Mike glanced at the shadows and saw the silent Earthmen standing there, watching. He saw them and suddenly he felt ashamed of Kerry and he looked away so that they should not see his face.

He took Kerry to the staircase and started up with him. He was sick twice more and he fell two or three times, too.

"What a crazy place to live," he muttered. "They're no better than worms, living underground like this. No better than worms. I'm telling you, Mike, if it wasn't for the fact that I knew you wouldn't like it I'd have killed the whole lot of them; I'd have just turned that needler on them. I'm telling you, Mike, they're not much better than animals."

Mike took hold of him and lifted him off the floor and they started up the stairs again.

With much waiting, pulling, helping, tugging, somehow Mike managed to get Kerry to the guardhouse. The guards eyed them oddly.

"Going out?"

"Yes—going back to our ship," said Mike.

"Going for good," said Kerry, wiping his mouth with his sleeve. "Never coming back to this damned hole, either. Going for good. For good..."

The bitter little breeze that had sprung up blew on Kerry and sobered him slightly. He stumbled a bit at first but soon they were walking quite quickly towards the ship, gleaming now, a silver pencil standing hidden by the trees, just glinting through them.

"There she is," said Kerry. "Boy, shall I be glad to get away from this place!" He turned and leered at Mike. "But you know what?"

"What?"

"We could have a helluva time here. With these needlers to back us, there isn't a thing on the planet that could stand up to us. Think of that, Mike, a whole planet to play with!"

"I've thought of it."

"Yes? I suppose you have. But it *is* a thought, isn't it? We could beat the mutants back and then live here—Lords of the Third Planet—Lord Mike and Lord Kerry, just like the stories in the Earth books."

They came near to the ship and the breeze blew little scattering showers of leaves about them as they walked towards it. Somewhere a song-thrush caroled; somewhere a cricket chirruped in the long grass.

"Guess I'm a bit tight, Mike. Can't seem to walk straight!" said Kerry.

"Never mind—we'll soon be gone. Rennig's up there waiting for us."

They started up the ladder.

"What do you think he'd say to this idea of stopping here?"

"I don't think he'd agree at all."

"No? Well, maybe you're right. I suppose he's too interested in exploring Earth. He's right, too, really. It'd be damned silly to stay here."

They reached the door and went in and climbed the second ladder up to the cabin, Mike in front, Kerry behind, climbing slowly.

"Well, here we are."

They stepped into the cabin and Kerry heaved a sigh, still swaying a little, still bug-eyed, still tight. Mike stood back and gently closed the door. Then Kerry saw Rennig.

"Great God! *Rennig!* What's happened?" He strode over and reached down, pulling Rennig upright and seeing the messy, sagging, burnt head. His hand came away and the scientist's body collapsed again like wet rubber.

Kerry stepped back and his eyes were opening and the dead look was fading from his face as light fades from the sky with night's coming. *"You* did this? He's been needled. Only you could have done it!"

Mike heard again all the old voices echoing in that one brief second before he answered, heard the two Mikes shouting their thoughts. The one telling him that he did right, the other condemning him for killing the man who had brought him to Earth, brought him home.

"Yes, Kerry."

"But God, man, *why?*"

"He was going to return to Venus. He told me he was going back to bring Venusians here to Earth. He wanted to make this place a Venusian colony. When I tried to stop him he threatened me with a needler. We struggled and he fell on his own weapon."

Kerry looked again at the body.

A silence came to the cabin. A stillness and a waiting, a cloying sense of something impending, something about to happen.

Kerry looked about at the wrecked instruments. "Did you do all this, too?"

"No. He did that. He wrecked the Automatic Control so that if we left we should have to work the ship on Manual and I should have to go with him and help. He did it purposely. He knew I should want to stay here."

Kerry turned quickly. "So you *do* want to stay?"

"Yes. I want to stay."

"Well, then, let's both stay."

"No, Kerry."

"What do you *mean?*" His voice came up. "What's the matter with you, Mike? What are you getting at?" He looked again at the slumped figure beside the wall. "You killed him. Without him you wouldn't be here. If it hadn't been for him you'd still be back on Venus in the green room, do you know that?"

"Yes, I know that."

"Then, good God, man, why did you do it—why did you kill him?"

"I told you it was an accident. Now stand over there against the wall" The needler shivered a little in Mike's hand. He steadied it.

"Mike, you don't know what you're doing! Put that needler down. Put it *down!*" Then he saw the look in his eyes and he knew that Mike would not put the needler down. He saw the angry glitter and the purposeful straight line of the mouth. And Kerry leapt sideways as the heat beam bit into the wall where he had been standing. He wrenched open the great door and flung himself down the ladder.

Mike's hand dropped. The needler fell to the floor. His eyes closed and dimly, dimly he heard Kerry going down the ladder to the door of the ship, heard the door opening, heard the duller sound of footsteps on the outside ladder. Then there was silence.

Then the little red band that had been holding him after that first shot snapped. He raced across the cabin and went down after Kerry. At the door he paused and looked out. He saw Kerry running in a queer, halting manner, way out among the trees. And he saw something else, too, amongst the trees.

A movement among the bushes, a rustling of the grass, something creeping, something evil.

He saw them clearly a minute later. There were two of them, both dwarfed, both ugly even from that distance. And Kerry had not yet seen them.

Mike started down the ladder and across the grass, the needler in his hand, held pointed, held steady.

He was too late. He fired as the first dwarf mutant lunged at Kerry with his spear. Kerry fell and lay still. Mike fired again, burning through the mutant's head. Then he pushed the button on the needler over to full power and scorched the second mutant to a small pile of cinders.

When he reached Kerry, Mike was breathing hard and he could not seem to see very clearly. He looked down and discovered that he was crying. The tears ran down his face and he made no effort to stop them. One fell on Kerry's white wax face.

Oh, yes, Kerry was quite, quite, dead.

CHAPTER FOURTEEN
Home

And that is how it all happened, how it came about.

Mike took the bodies of Kerry and Rennig and buried them in a lonely place. There is nothing to show that two Venusians had come except the ship, and that is rusty and alone now. Mike sealed shut the great door and destroyed the ladder and the ship is a silent monument, a monolith of slowly oxidizing metal.

And the Others are frightened now. There have been two more battles, and the Earthmen, with their M.V. guns, their Bygrave Burner and their needlers have won each time. The Others have indeed become frightened and have started to move away from the hills about the plateau, out into the desert land to the south.

Mike has changed the way of life of the Earth people, too. They no longer live their lives under the earth, for Mike proved to them that the Others were afraid of the strange new weapons. And now they have built a great wooden fence about the plateau and are building houses within it. Soon there will be quite a little village there. And some of the men want to move away and start another village in a nearby valley.

But more important than all this, more important than the going of the mutants and the enterprise of the Earthmen is the thing that is growing in the minds of Mike and Willa and

Gray and all of them, the knowledge that the human race is a great race and may one day be as once it was.

The only things that Mike took from the ship were the guns and the great Earth books that he had brought with him from Venus. And he and Gray and old Willa read them often by the firelight and marvel at the things that were.

Sometimes Mike goes up to the hill above the city and sits on the brow for a long time (for there is no fear of attack now), and he gazes at the city as he did on that first day—- waiting for the time when the people will return; when the plague shall be burnt away. And he knows that though he will never see it, that time will surely come.

And it is at times like that that he gets to thinking of Rennig and Kerry. And the two little Mikes start arguing all over again about whether he did the right thing or not. But in his heart he knows the answer, in the same way that Willa must have known the answer when she let her son be burnt to save her people.

And sometimes, too, at evening, he looks up at the sky and roves the stars with his eyes until he sees, bright in the heavens, a shining point of diamond brilliance, the evening star that is Venus. And no sigh escapes him; no thought of regret flits through his mind; no longing for that other world, so far lost in space and time.

Then it is that he turns and makes his way back to the stockade and the growing little village, and the rusty light from the wood fire; and then he sniffs in the earthy, leafy smell of *home* and he is glad.

THE END